WITHDRAWN

ALIEN SUMMER

For Colton—CS

PENGUIN WORKSHOP
An imprint of Penguin Random House LLC, New York

First published in the United States of America by Penguin Workshop,
an imprint of Penguin Random House LLC, New York, 2022

Text copyright © 2022 by James S. Murray and Carsen Smith
Illustrations copyright © 2022 by Penguin Random House LLC

Insert illustrations by Patrick Spaziante

Insert HUD assets: NatalyaBurova/iStock/Getty Images, Nattapon Kongbunmee/iStock/Getty
Images, PlargueDoctor/iStock/Getty Images, SerGRAY/iStock/Getty Images, St_Aurora72/
iStock/Getty Images, Veronika Oliinyk/iStock/Getty Images

Visit us online at penguinrandomhouse.com.

Library of Congress Cataloging-in-Publication Data is available.

Manufactured in Canada

ISBN 9780593226124   10 9 8 7 6 5 4 3 2 1 FRI

AREA·51 INTERNS
ALIEN SUMMER

BY JAMES S. MURRAY
AND CARSEN SMITH

PENGUIN WORKSHOP

CHAPTER ONE

"KEEP GOING! DON'T LOOK BACK!"

Vivian Harlow wanted to stop and find a place to hide, but the sound of explosions mixing with her mom's commanding voice told her to keep moving. Around her, the few humans still standing attempted to hold off the horde of alien creatures that had overtaken the world's most top secret military base—Area 51.

Vivian nervously scanned the room; it was massive, and she couldn't remember the way out. Viv ran as fast as her legs could carry her, looking for a door or an exit sign . . . anything that could lead her to safety and out of this chaos. But someone—or some*thing*—rushed up behind her. Before she could react, whatever had been chasing her grabbed ahold of her shoulder and pushed her against the wall.

Viv's head whipped back, and she saw her mom's face. A wave of relief washed over her, and all she wanted was to jump into her mother's arms and hug her, but she knew there wasn't time.

She watched as her mom frantically punched a code into the control panel on a low air vent along the back wall. The door to the airshaft unlocked with a clunk, and the metal gate flung open.

"Quick! Get in and start crawling!" she shouted at Viv, fighting to be heard over the roaring booms and explosions. She lifted Viv into the open airshaft.

"But what about you? You can't fit in here! I'm not leaving you!" Viv cried out as her body tumbled into the tight air duct. The icy metal of the vent burned against Viv's skin as she tried to climb back up. The lights from the hall bounced off the platinum walls that now surrounded her.

Viv squinted up at her mom, and their eyes locked. "I'll be okay," her mom said. "Your friends are already in the airshaft. Go look after them." For the first time in her life, Viv could see her mother was frightened. Viv's jaw trembled, but before she could choke a few last words out, her mom's body was wrenched backward by some unseen force.

"NOOO!" Viv screamed, struggling to climb back out of the airshaft.

She froze in horror as she saw her mom levitating over a pile of unconscious bodies. Her arms dangled by her sides, and her whole body went limp.

Nearby, Viv could see one of the creatures with its arm extended, using its mind to hold her mom in the air telekinetically.

Viv took in the creatures, the *aliens*, in their true form.

Standing three times the size of any human, they were utterly terrifying. And there were dozens of them.

Viv didn't know what to do. She desperately wanted to climb out of the air vent and save her mom, but how could one kid stop all these aliens?

Around the room, the aliens began to rise toward the ceiling, their eyes scanning for any remaining humans. One turned in her direction. Viv couldn't tell if it saw her or not, but a frightened squeak escaped her throat as she ducked back into the vent. The creature floated past without stopping.

Close call.

The others were already in the airshaft, and she had to find them. Scurrying farther along the metal floor, she found her two friends huddling and terrified. Charlotte and Ray sat motionless. Their eyes filled with tears as they looked to Viv.

"What do we do, Viv?" Charlotte asked, her voice low and trembling.

They're waiting for me to take charge . . .

But I'm just as scared as they are!

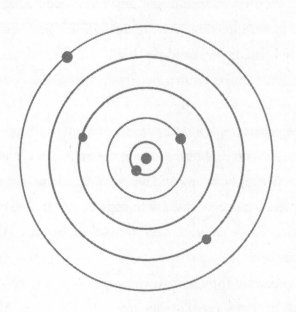

CHAPTER TWO

ONE DAY EARLIER . . .

Viv stared into her locker for the last time. All around her, she could hear the other students of Groom Lake Middle School celebrating, throwing pencil cases into the air and tearing up essays. She pulled off the Marvel comic book covers that lined the sides of her locker like wallpaper. Her vintage postcard of computer scientist Alan Turing had faded over the past year, but she stashed it in her backpack, anyway. Finally, one by one, she peeled off the dozens of astronomy stickers that covered the locker door.

A photo of Albert Einstein sticking his tongue out came loose and fluttered past her.

As she bent down to pick it up, her locker door slammed shut just above her head.

"BOO!"

"AH!"

Viv clutched her heart and looked up to see a familiar wave of snowy-blond hair.

"HAH!" Charlotte cackled, her icy-blue eyes sparkling. "You should've seen your face! You look like you peed your pants!"

"Geez, Charlotte! Don't scare me like that!" Viv shouted.

"Wait. *Did* you pee your pants?"

"What? No!" Viv replied, though she couldn't help her cheeks getting red with embarrassment.

Charlotte let out a big snort. It was so loud that other kids in the hallway turned their heads to stare. She had always been a bit of an oddball, and it didn't help that she'd inherited a slight Australian accent from her dad that made her loud voice stand out even more. Nobody at school really appreciated Charlotte's brashness. But to Viv, she was wonderfully weird and awkward in all the right ways.

"It's summer vacation, baby! Are you stoked or what?" Charlotte exclaimed.

"Oh yeah! Totally!" Viv replied, smiling half-heartedly. As glad as she was to be done with classes and homework for the summer, she couldn't deny that the thought of leaving middle school—and her friends—was freaking her out.

"Well, you better be excited," Charlotte continued. "Because next year you're going to that boring school for magnets."

"It's not a school for magnets, it's a magnet school. As in, a specialized high school for kids that are good in math and science."

"Is it called a magnet school because it pulls you away from all your friends?"

"No," Viv replied. "Or . . . ugh . . . maybe."

"Well, I know what I'm going to do this summer," Charlotte said, twirling her hair between her fingers. "I'm finally gonna master playing guitar with my feet!"

Last week, when Viv was over at Charlotte's house for dinner, she found a welcome pamphlet from Bartram School for the Arts, a school for musically talented students. It came as no surprise that Charlotte had been accepted. She was the best guitar player Viv had ever seen, and was already so good at playing regularly that strumming with her toes had become her latest obsession. Viv was happy her friend was following her dreams, but deep down Viv wondered if their friendship could survive four years apart.

"Plus, this summer we *have* to plan you the best thirteenth birthday party!" Charlotte pretended to wipe a tear. "You're finally growing up!"

"Hey!" Viv said, "It's not my fault I started kindergarten early! You know my mom—"

"STOP RIGHT THERE, YOUNG MAN!"

A high-pitched voice bounced off the metal lockers and clanged in Viv's ears. A screech like that could only be coming from one source—Mrs. Agner, the crotchety old geography teacher.

Viv turned toward the commotion, and a disheveled young

boy darted toward them in a whirlwind of flailing arms and ill-fitting clothes. "It wasn't me, I swear!" the boy cried. "I'm an innocent man! I was framed!"

Viv quickly sidestepped as the boy brushed past her, sending her curly black hair fluttering.

"GET BACK HERE THIS INSTANT!" Mrs. Agner roared after him, clomping down the hallway in her bright green heels.

After a few moments of muffled shouting, Mrs. Agner walked back in their direction, with the young boy marching dejectedly by her side. He let out a heavy breath as his scruffy brown hair flopped over his fogged-up glasses.

At eleven years old, Ray Mond was the youngest kid in the entire eighth-grade class, but he was also the smartest. He was Viv's next-door neighbor, and they had been traveling to school together every day since he had skipped a few grades in elementary school. Viv had hoped that Ray would be going to her magnet school, too, but her mom had hinted that his family couldn't afford it, which Viv found strange, considering Ray's dad and her mom both worked at the same place.

"I'm telling you, I'm a scapegoat! It's all a setup!" Ray shouted, trying to reason with the infuriated Mrs. Agner. She finally let go of her vise grip and whipped around to face the shaking boy.

"Mr. Mond!" the fuming teacher said. "You're lucky if I don't suspend you right now!"

"Technically, since the bell already rang *and* it's the last day of school, we're all suspended until September," Ray whispered under his breath.

Mrs. Agner turned cherry red. Viv braced for the explosion, but there was no arguing with Ray's logic. She marched off with a huff that sort of sounded like a deflating koala bear.

"Ray!" Charlotte said. "What'd you do that made her so angry?"

Ray took a few deep breaths and tucked his wrinkled shirt into the waistband of his underpants, which were riding up a few inches higher than his pants.

"I was in the physics lab testing out the propulsion capabilities of my meatball catapult. It's not my fault that she didn't read the 'Experiment in Progress' sign!"

He pointed toward Mrs. Agner, who was still stomping down the hallway. Sure enough, caught in a chunk of her frizzy red locks on the back of her head was a fair amount of marinara sauce and chopped meat.

"Oh, I forgot to mention," Ray continued. "The catapult works! First meatball to break the sound barrier."

"Good on ya, mate!" Charlotte exclaimed.

"My next experiment—to see if a meatball can break the speed of light!" Ray said. "I swear, sometimes the teachers in this school just don't understand genius when they see it."

"Says the boy who thinks time travel is real," Charlotte teased.

"It is!" Ray declared. "It's 10:30 p.m. in London right now. That's the *future*!"

"Time zones and time travel aren't the same thing, Ray!"

Ray blinked at Charlotte.

"Just you wait until I finish building my time portal this summer," Ray said. "Then *I'll* be the one laughing when I'm having a cup of tea with Leonardo da Vinci!"

Viv couldn't help but smile. As smart as Ray was, sometimes he could get a little carried away.

"Anyway, you guys excited for tomorrow or what?!" Ray asked.

Viv looked back at him with a raised brow.

Huh? What's happening tomorrow?

"Hey, over there! You three!"

Viv spun on her heels to see some of the baseball team calling out to the trio. She recognized the faces of Will, Gabe, and Colin as they motioned toward her and her friends from the nearby water fountain.

But it was another face in the team huddle that made Viv's heart flutter.

Elijah Padilla. Viv's ultimate crush since third grade. To Viv, he was Clark Kent, Peter Parker, and Bruce Wayne combined into one boy. Except without any of the superpowers, spiderwebs, and billions of dollars. But still. He was perfect to her.

"You guys coming to the lake tomorrow?" Will asked. "Everyone's gonna be there!" Viv couldn't believe her ears.

She and Charlotte rarely got invited to hang out after school. And Ray? Viv wasn't sure if he'd ever been to a party in his entire life. Especially not parties at the *lake*.

Viv felt her knees start to go weak. She imagined spending the whole day with Elijah, his jet-black hair wet and sandy. Watching the sunset on the shore as the waves washed over their feet . . .

"Ahh, sorry. We can't go tomorrow!" Charlotte answered.

"Yeah," Ray butted in, "we get to go with our parents to Take Your Kids to Work Day!"

Viv's daydream evaporated.

Aw, man. I completely forgot about that. Mom's been talking about it for weeks.

The baseball boys down the hall scoffed among themselves, except for Elijah, who just turned away to open his locker, adjusting the collar on his signature leather Air Force jacket.

"Oh, right. Have fun at that crummy theme park!" Will mocked.

Ray retreated behind Charlotte, but still managed to shout back, "It's not a theme park—it's Area 51! One of the top science facilities in the country!"

"Really? Then explain the busloads of tourists, the gift shop, and the food carts?" Colin asked. "Sounds like a theme park to me."

"Yeah! Don't forget your pointy alien ears," Gabe added. "And bring me back a churro!"

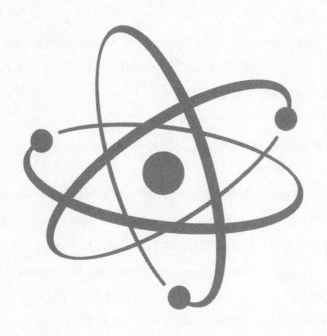

CHAPTER THREE

THE NEXT DAY . . .

"Surprise!"

Cassandra Harlow slid a full plate of breakfast in front of her daughter, cheery despite the ungodly hour. It was 5:30 a.m. on Saturday, earlier than Viv ever had to be up for school. She was utterly exhausted, rubbing at her eyes like she was trying to erase them.

Viv stared at the mess on the dish, taking a few seconds to realize the food clumsily spelled out *51*. The number *1* looked right: a long strip of bacon. Hard to mess that up. But the number *5* looked like a half-eaten pancake with a few microwavable sausages around it. Viv had dissected frogs in biology class that looked more appetizing.

"What do you think? Do you like it?" Cassandra asked cheerily.

"It, uh . . . looks great, Mom." Viv murmured.

Viv's mom had never been a great cook, but Viv knew she

did the best she could, considering she was a single parent who worked a high-stress job. From time to time, Viv would daydream about the father she had never met. She wondered what the breakfasts he cooked looked like. She decided he liked to make cheesy egg omelets that melted in your mouth with a side of grapefruit topped with sugar.

Cassandra was already dressed in a full pantsuit, clearly energized. Viv, on the other hand, felt like a potato that just got run over by a monster truck.

"Ugh," Viv groaned. "How long do I have to be there?" She stabbed one of the breakfast sausages with her fork.

"Well, honey, it is Take Your Kids to Work *Day*. So I imagine that we'll be there all day!" her mom declared, scrubbing her own dish in the sink.

"But everybody else is going to the lake today . . . ," Viv complained, chewing on a half-hearted bite of pancake. It tasted like a wet napkin.

"I know, baby. But today you get to walk a mile in my shoes, see what I do for a living. This is a once-in-a-lifetime experience!"

"Going to a party at the lake is a once-in-a-lifetime experience," Viv replied. "I can watch you give tours to a bunch of alien conspiracy theorists any day."

"Oh, Viv. You know that's not what I do. Your mom works at one of the coolest places in the world! And once I step onto that base, it's like a whirlwind. Remember, Viv, I *am* the director of futur—"

"Director of future technology. Whatever that means. I just don't know why it *had* to be today, and not, you know, in the *future* . . ."

Cassandra took a seat at the table. "I'm sorry, Viv," she said, leaning in to give her a kiss on the forehead. "Let's just get to the base, and then we'll see how it goes."

Viv sighed and then pasted on a smile. Even if she was annoyed to miss going to the lake, she knew how important today was for her mom.

Cassandra brushed some hair behind her daughter's ear. Then in one quick motion, she pulled her car key from her pocket and pressed the Unlock button.

From the driveway, the loud car horn broke the silence of the morning. Neighborhood dogs barked and howled in a chorus.

"Ready to roll?"

"What?! I'm not even dressed!"

"Don't worry, Viv," her mom replied. "Just messing with you. Today the US government waits for *us*." Her mother laughed, flashing Viv a huge smile. "Meet me outside when you're ready."

Viv choked down the rest of the papery pancake before heading to her room to throw on a navy blue T-shirt and some ripped jeans. She laced up her sneakers and bounded out the door, ready to weather whatever the day had to offer.

The Area 51 compound was a run-down collection of old buildings, dusty launchpads, overgrown landing fields, and rusted plane hangars. Outside the main gates was a mini village of gift shops, food trucks, and parking lots filled with tour buses. A sign on the side of the road read "Future Site of Chipotle." A huge green plastic alien waved at passersby, with a cheesy "Welcome Earthlings!" banner above its head.

The kids at school were right. It was like someone had built a crummy Disney World in the desert for space geeks.

Viv peeked out the window. A line of tourists already stood there, snapping photos of the fake miniature flying saucer "crashed" into the ground. One of the photo takers accidentally backed up into a hot dog stand, sending a tray of corn dogs careening into the dirt. Before anyone noticed, the clumsy tourist sneakily picked one up and took a big, sandy bite.

Viv slouched down in her seat, praying that no one could see her, not that she thought any of the kids from school would be caught dead anywhere near this place.

"I know what you're thinking," Cassandra said as they approached the main gate. "But it's a lot more impressive on the inside."

They stopped at a security checkpoint, and Viv watched as her mom exchanged pleasantries with two soldiers—it was still a government building, after all. It was weird seeing her mom at work. Viv knew her mom had a life outside their home, but it felt strange to see her in business mode instead of breakfast mode.

Viv peered at what she thought was the main building: a stacked multiplex of disc-like buildings. But something else farther in the distance caught her eye.

What's that huge dome?

"Oh, look who's here!" her mother said excitedly as they rounded the final turn toward the front gate.

Leaning against a familiar beaten-up sedan parked out front, Ray struggled to hold up a big beach umbrella. He had splotches of sunscreen applied sloppily all over his face, like his head was a pizza made out of whipped cream.

"Why does Ray look like that?" Viv asked.

"I know how badly you wanted to go to the lake today, so I have a little surprise for you and your friends," Viv's mom replied.

"Howdy, Harlows!"

The booming voice clapped through the air as a sweaty man popped out of the sedan's driver's-side door. It was Ray's dad, Mr. Al Mond, who stood at least a foot shorter than Director Harlow.

Viv had known him as her next-door neighbor practically her whole life. But today, he was wearing something different as he stepped out of the car, definitely not the usual T-shirt and cargo shorts he wore mowing his lawn.

Viv read the badge on Mr. Mond's jumpsuit. "Chief Custodial Officer."

Custodial? Like . . . mops?

Considering how inventive Ray was, Viv had always assumed his dad was a scientist of some kind. Only now did she realize she had never asked before.

"Hi, Al, good to see you," Viv's mom said. "Thank you so much for agreeing to take the kids out to the lake!"

"Oh, not a problem, Director! Always happy to help!" Mr. Mond eagerly replied.

Viv looked up at her mother in disbelief.

"So wait . . . I *am* going to the lake after all?" Viv asked.

"Surprise! I thought about what you said, and you're right. I texted Al on our way over." Her mom placed a loving hand on Viv's shoulder. "You should spend the first day of summer with friends. So we'll do a half day at the base today, and then Mr. Mond will drive you kids to the lake to have fun with your friends."

"Really?" Viv asked, trying to contain her excitement.

"Yes, really," her mom replied with a grin.

Viv's daydream returned and flooded her senses. She imagined Elijah in a Hawaiian shirt, smiling and waving in her direction, the tides of the lake rolling in behind him. The desert breeze floated past, tossing his hair into a perfect mess.

A door slammed behind her, snapping Viv out of her trance. A tall man wearing a crisp business suit marched out of the base's entrance and straight toward Director Harlow.

"Oh, Brooks! Perfect timing," Viv's mom said.

"Director Harlow, yes," the mysterious man said, a bit

flustered. "I hate to hurry you, but everyone is here, and the presentation—"

"Yes, yes, Brooks." Director Harlow cut him off. "No need to rush on such a special day! Viv, Ray, this is Mr. Brooks Yates, assistant director of the compound and my trusty second-in-command. He's one of our best. Young, brilliant, and full of ambition. Reminds me of myself when I was younger."

Mr. Yates's expression switched into a big smile. He swiveled to face the two kids.

"That's so kind of you to say, Director. And speaking of, where are my manners? This must be the famous Vivian Harlow."

He crouched down, coming face-to-face with Viv and staring at her with a piercing gaze. The peppermint smell was so strong on his breath that it almost burned Viv's eyes.

"Your name is Brooks Yates?" Ray asked curiously. "Does everyone in your family have two plural names?"

"Ray!" Mr. Mond chuckled nervously, nudging his son in the shoulder.

Mr. Yates turned his gaze to the short, precocious boy with a face full of smudged sunblock and let out a perturbed huff.

"Well, kids," Director Harlow cut in, hastily changing the subject, "regardless of his name, you have Mr. Yates to thank for today. Area 51's first ever Take Your Kids to Work Day was his brilliant idea."

"Yes, of course. Inspiring the future scientists of tomorrow!" Mr. Yates said quickly.

"Are your kids already inside, Brooks?" Director Harlow asked.

"Oh no, they couldn't make it. Still a bit too young for any of this, I'm afraid. Shall we?" Mr. Yates proposed, motioning toward the door.

"After you!" Director Harlow motioned back.

"Ready to get our SCIENCE on?" Ray whispered, elbowing Viv and smiling at her with a mouth full of braces. Viv chuckled and punched him in the arm in return.

"Ow! What the heck was that for?!" Ray clutched his arm, dropping the heavy umbrella with a thud.

"Let's go get our science on, dork!" Viv said.

With Mr. Yates leading the way, Viv and Ray followed their parents and entered through the gates of Area 51 for the first time in their lives.

CHAPTER FOUR

Viv had pictured her mother's office a million times, imagining it as a hub of high-tech excellence fit for the director of the base. But this place looked more boring than anything she could have imagined.

The walls were painted a dingy beige, and the entire room was filled with row after row of old desktop computers and squeaky rolling chairs. A huge copy machine chugged along, spitting out pages of documents next to a half-empty water cooler. The tourists outside who were dying to get into this place probably imagined jetpacks, 3D printers, and laser guns.

But now Viv knew the truth. It was just another dull, corporate office space. She sighed.

I guess a part of me was hoping that the space geeks were right . . .

"Aw, man," Ray whispered to Viv, clearly having the same thoughts. He lifted a churro to his mouth and took a bite.

"When'd you find time to get a churro?" Viv whispered back.

"Honestly, I don't remember. Want a bite?" He extended the fried stick toward his friend.

"Ray, it's eight in the morning!"

"You're right. I'll save the rest for lunch." He wiped his mouth and stowed the half-eaten churro in the back pocket of his jeans.

After her mother set down her things in her office, they headed to a large conference room on the main floor that looked just as drab as the rest of the building. The room was filled with other Area 51 employees and their kids, most of them from other schools in the Groom Lake area. Viv scanned the crowd until she finally found a familiar face.

Charlotte stood beside her mom and dad, seeing as she had a double whammy of Area 51 parents. Her mother, Dr. Sabrina Frank, was tall and stoic, but her father, Mr. Desmond Frank, was a smiling blond man with a faint scar above his left temple. Viv had always wondered if the scar was from some top secret weapon malfunction or from an alien switchblade. Now it seemed like the most dangerous thing in this room was a stapler.

Viv could feel the hair on her arms stand up. A familiar sight caught her eye from the back of the room.

No way . . . It can't be.

A leather Air Force jacket. Black hair. Brown eyes. It was . . .

Elijah! What is he doing here?

But he wasn't alone. Walking next to him, matching him strut for strut, was his father. Viv squinted toward the name tag on the man's jacket: "Lt. Nicolás Padilla." He wore a bigger version of the Air Force leather jacket that Elijah had on, and Viv recalled Elijah mentioning his dad had served in the Air Force for a while before settling down.

Viv's heart thudded in her chest.

Whoa . . . Elijah's dad works here, too? No way. I can't believe he's here instead of at the lake!

Before she could calm her nerves, Lieutenant Padilla called out to her.

"Ah, you must be Vivian Harlow!" His smile was blindingly white. "I've heard a lot about you, young lady."

Heard a lot about me? But that must mean . . .

Viv glanced over at Elijah. His eyes were suddenly glued to the floor.

Is he . . . blushing?

"Come on, Dad! Let's get a good seat," Elijah suggested, practically dragging his father by the arm over to the rows of chairs set up in the middle of the conference hall.

When Viv turned back around, she realized her mom had already walked toward the center of the hall to deliver the welcome speech. Director Harlow stepped onto a raised wooden platform and up to the rickety podium. She leaned in to speak into the old, dented microphone.

"Good morning, everyone!" Director Harlow said confidently.

Her employees answered enthusiastically, "Good morning, Director Harlow!"

"I'm glad everyone was able to find a seat, even when there's a few more of us here than normal." She motioned toward the group as Viv awkwardly slid into the only empty seat remaining, next to Charlotte.

"We're very excited to have all you kids here for Take Your Kids to Work Day. Now, I know for most of you students, it's the first day of summer, and the last thing you want to do is spend a day with your *parents*. Or even just half a day . . ."

She winked at Vivian, and Viv smiled in return.

"So first, how about a quick, fun history lesson?" Vivian's mom was beaming; she was completely in her element. "And before you pull out your cell phones because you're bored, just know—the base has a built-in jammer that disables any visitors' devices."

Viv looked at her cell phone, and sure enough, it wouldn't turn on, no matter what button she pressed. Charlotte let out a low groan, quiet enough for Viv and Ray to hear but loud enough to make her own mom shush her.

Viv glanced up and caught Elijah's eye from across the room for just a second before they both quickly looked away. Viv awkwardly tucked her hair behind her ears and fixed her eyes on the floor. Her mom's commanding voice cut through the tension.

Charlotte's hand shot up in the air. Viv's mom was caught off guard by the sudden question.

"Um, yes? Charlotte?"

"That's great and all . . . but what the heck do you guys actually *do* here?" Charlotte asked. "I've been asking my parents for years, and I never get a straight answer."

Every adult in the room laughed. The kids looked at one another nervously.

"Well, that's a very good question, Charlotte. Some people think we test out nuclear weapons here. Some people think we use this base for highly classified government experiments, or time travel, or warp technology. You've probably seen all of the movies and TV shows about this place. They say we're the ones who study and possess extraterrestrial life-forms."

"This is it!" Ray nudged Viv, sprinkling little bits of churro sugar dust from his mouth. "Here comes the cool stuff!"

"But the presentation we have for you today is way more exciting than all of that nonsense!"

"Holy moly, I can't wait!" Ray could barely contain himself. If his fingers hadn't been covered in a crusty layer of cinnamon, he might actually have looked adorable.

Director Harlow turned to the side of the podium. "Brooks, if you don't mind?"

Her second-in-command, Mr. Yates, popped another Tic Tac into his mouth and uncomfortably shimmied his way onto the podium. Reaching into his suit pocket, he pulled out a small panel with a large red button.

"Over the last few weeks, our team has been working very hard to push the boundaries of science. Today, we're excited to announce that our latest project is finally up and running. And fully functional!"

"I'm telling you, they built a freaking Death Star!" Ray whispered to no one in particular.

A stained off-color projector screen descended from the ceiling behind Mr. Yates. "As you know, many of us here at Area 51 love outer space," he said, clearing his throat before continuing. "And while not all of us can be astronauts . . . or pass the physical fitness examination you need to become an astronaut . . ."

Geez. Getting pretty personal here.

"That doesn't mean our dreams of interstellar life are hopeless. Which is why our team of scientists has figured out a way to . . ." Mr. Yates pressed the red button, lighting up the big projector in the back of the room. "Grow coconuts . . . in space!"

Viv stared up at the projection screen. The graphic showed a floating hydroponic garden beside the International Space Station. Small palm trees sprouted out of the rows of plastic planters. All the kids in the audience sat there in confused silence. The Area 51 employees erupted into applause.

Charlotte let out a scoff. Ray's arms dropped down by his side.

"What?" he whispered to Viv. "Uh . . . That's it? A coconut garden?"

Director Harlow pointed back toward the image. "We've discovered a way to grow these normally tropical plants in the cold, harsh vacuum of space. Our primary plant is expected to produce its first coconut in a little over two years! Pretty cool, huh? Imagine that—astronauts will soon be able to make *space smoothies!*"

Ray pouted next to Viv. "My catapult could have shot a coconut to the space station for half the price. That's so lame." Viv let out a sigh, too.

Even I was expecting something a little more impressive . . .

"Okay, so if that gives you any idea, you're gonna have a lot of fun today! Parents—please pair up with your kids, and, kids, stick close to your parents! And remember, although we can't show you the *entire* base, everything that you will see and hear is highly classified. So no sharing stories later with your other friends on TockClock!"

Ray leaned into Viv's ear. "Your mom's the director of future technology, and she thinks TikTok is called *TockClock*?"

"Future technology. Not current technology," Viv replied.

Ray huffed, pulled the churro out of his pocket, and took another big bite. Viv mentally geared herself up for what was sure to be an incredibly dull few hours as her mom made her final address.

"Everyone, enjoy your day and without further ado, welcome to Area Fif—"

Suddenly, a high-pitched alarm cut her off, and emergency lights along the ceiling flashed bright red. The shrill tone echoed through the main hall. Ray covered his ears with his hands.

Something's not right.

"Wh-what's going on?" Charlotte asked. "Are the coconuts okay?"

For a moment, Viv saw a flash of fear pass over her mother's face. If *she* was scared, then they were in deep trouble.

The watch on Director Harlow's wrist joined in the chorus of alarms. She scrolled through the alerts, and half a second later, her expression turned serious. Determined.

"Deactivate the cloaking system now!" Director Harlow commanded.

"But the kids are here!" Charlotte's dad protested.

"There's no time! Do it now!"

Mr. Frank rushed over to the wall and elbowed a panel. The section of plaster flipped up, revealing a control pad of hundreds of buttons. He entered a quick combination and slammed down on a lever.

In the blink of an eye, the entire room transformed. Sleek steel now lined nearly every inch of the place. And whatever wasn't made of steel was immaculate glass so thick, it must've been bulletproof. The cracked tiles on the floor spun beneath Viv's feet, revealing dark gray floors lit up with glowing LED arrows of a thousand different colors. Dashboards that radiated bright blue and red lights emerged from every desk. It was truly magnificent.

Ray spat his churro out onto the floor.

What? What the heck is happening?

The compound suddenly looked exactly the way she'd imagined it all those years, the way the tourists and fanatics outside imagined it. The other kids in the room let out sharp gasps.

"Mom?!" Viv called out. But Director Harlow had already jumped off the podium.

"Brooks, engage the internal lockdown procedure!" she ordered.

"Yes, ma'am!" Mr. Yates hurried over to a glass monitor that extended from the wall.

Every screen around the room blazed to life. Each monitor flashed a blinking map of the compound, showing a field of big red dots rounding the corner of an underground labyrinth. The dots were growing larger . . . and rapidly moving toward the main hall . . . *where they were all standing.*

Quickly, Viv's mom sprang into action. She rushed over to the flat computer panel on the wall that read "CENTRAL BRAIN" and plunged her hand into a blue orb of light. A red scanning beam passed over her arm, processing her handprint. The orb of light turned from blue to green.

"Pull up security cameras for Quadrant 2B, subsectors 413 through 6JW!"

Instantly, a previously hidden floating panel of twenty hologram screens extended from the back wall. Each screen showed a different cell of what appeared to be a super-high-tech underground prison. Viv's mom frantically scrolled through the touch-screen holograms. After a few seconds, she pulled up a video stream showing what looked like a glass holding tank . . . but the glass had been shattered outward.

"Oh *no*." Her face went pale. "Brooks, any luck with that lockdown?"

"It's not working!" Mr. Yates called out, desperately pressing buttons on the security screen.

Everyone else in the hall was as still as a statue. Employees protectively wrapped their arms around their kids. Viv slowly rose from her chair and cautiously approached her mother.

This can't be real. None of this can be real. Is this some kind of prank?

"Mom? What's happening?" she shouted over the emergency sirens.

Director Harlow looked down at her daughter, real panic spreading across her face.

"The aliens from planet ZR-18 . . . *They've escaped.*"

CHAPTER FIVE

. . . Aliens?

Even after all the jokes about Area 51 and her own hopes that her mother was a part of something more important than just space coconuts, Viv had never actually believed that aliens were real. She still couldn't really believe it—but the expression on Director Harlow's face couldn't be a lie. She looked pale and terrified, like a ghost who had just seen an even scarier ghost.

For a split second, everything was quiet in the main hall. Agents, engineers, and employees who had apparently trained their whole lives for a moment like this stood deathly still. Fear hung heavy in the air. Viv felt a familiar grip on her hand.

"This should never have happened. I'm sorry, Viv. You were never meant to find out about any of this."

Director Harlow wrapped her arm around Viv's shoulders and held her so close, Viv could feel her mother's pounding heartbeat. Director Harlow glanced down at her watch.

"We're too late. They're here."

BOOM! BOOM! BOOM!

Everyone's head whipped around. A set of titanium doors along the side of the room rattled ferociously. It sounded like a stampede of elephants slamming into the door repeatedly. Ray let out a scared yelp. All eyes were on the doors' bending, clattering frame.

Viv's fists clenched. Panic shot through her body.

It's true. All the rumors are true. This place . . .

Suddenly, the banging on the door stopped. It went silent.

A human hand appeared from behind the door. A set of long fingers curled around the frame and slowly creaked it open. The door swung out completely, revealing the silhouette of a giant man. His shadowy figure turned to color as he stepped out of the darkness into the bright lights of the main hall.

He wore a long khaki-colored trench coat and a matching fedora, and a scratchy five-o'clock shadow grew on the edges of his chin. His walk was unnaturally smooth, almost as if he was gliding across the floor. The brim of his hat cut across the top of his face.

"Wait . . . *that's* an alien?" Charlotte whispered under her breath. "He dresses like Grandpa!"

"They've transformed themselves to look like humans," Charlotte's mom whispered back. "It's a cloaking mechanism. That's not their true form."

Viv gulped. *They can do that? Then what else can they do?*

The mysterious man lifted his head to survey the room. Viv's heart pounded in her chest. Now she could see the only thing about him that was clearly not human: His eyes were glowing. And not the way she thought Elijah's eyes glowed . . . This man's eyes were a glaring, bright fluorescent green.

His shoes clacked across the metal floor. As he made his way toward the people in the back of the room, Viv felt her mom tug on her sleeve. Director Harlow knelt down to her daughter's level.

"Listen closely. Hold on to your friends and stay right behind me," Director Harlow whispered.

Viv followed her instructions. She grabbed Charlotte's and Ray's hands and tightly squeezed through the crowd of terrified employees and the other kids. Director Harlow shuffled them along the edge of the wall and toward the back of the room. Just as they huddled against an air vent in the corner, a booming voice filled the hall.

"Well, what do you know? All my favorite people in one place." The man's voice was deep and scratchy. He had a peculiar accent, like someone from those old black-and-white movies.

That's *how aliens sound?*

"Stay hidden. And stay low," Viv's mom instructed the kids. She stepped out through the crowded mass of employees toward the strange man.

"Mom! *No! Don't* leave us!" Viv begged.

"Where are you? I can hear you whispering back there,"

the mysterious alien called out. "Director Harlow? I *know* you're in here."

"Megdar, I understand that you're angry." Director Harlow's voice echoed through the hall. Viv looked to her mother, confused.

Megdar? They know each other?

"Angry?" Megdar laughed. "Who said anything about me being angry?"

Megdar patrolled the edge of the crowd, searching for Director Harlow among the hundreds of faces.

"Why don't you show yourself, and we'll see how angry I get?" He beckoned.

"I know your time here as our guests hasn't been the most comfortab—"

"Oh, so now we're your guests?" Megdar stalked back and forth.

"You've always been guests on this planet," Director Harlow insisted.

"Forgive me. Perhaps my understanding of the English language has gotten worse over the last few decades," Megdar mused. "But my fellow Roswellians and I consider ourselves more like your *prisoners*."

Viv's ears perked up at his words.

Roswellians? Prisoners?

"Isn't that right, everyone?" Megdar motioned toward the bent door frame.

Suddenly, dozens of others Roswellians piled into the main hall. Viv tried counting them but lost track after fifty. They were all dressed in old-fashioned clothing. The women wore pleated dresses, and the men wore suspenders and long slacks. Everyone in the room was now surrounded by the army of aliens, all with the same glowing green eyes as their leader.

"Name your price, Megdar. Anything you want. Weapons? Technology? I can get you anything you need," Director Harlow offered. "Please. Just leave this place in peace."

Megdar laughed to himself. "You know what I want. Something you took from me a long time ago. Give it to me, and we'll leave in peace."

"I assure you that I don't know what you're talking about. But I'm sure we can work out a deal," Director Harlow replied.

"You and I both know that's not true, Cassandra," he hissed. "The *progeny* is here in this building. Right now. I can sense it. We can all sense it."

"The progeny?" Director Harlow asked. "I'm sorry, but I don't know what you mean."

"Don't lie. Of course you do," Megdar replied through gritted teeth, his fingers tightly clenching. "That's all we want. Right, guys?"

For a split second, Megdar turned his back, looking to his alien army for support.

"NOW!" Director Harlow called out.

Charlotte's dad instantly made his move. He whipped open

his jacket, revealing a holster belt with half a dozen different futuristic guns. In a flash, he ripped a high-tech-looking blaster from its strap, aimed the weapon, and pulled the trigger.

A bright blue laser shot out of the barrel at lightning speed. The beam flew through the air—directly at Megdar's head.

Megdar snapped his hand up, freezing the beam in midair. It all happened so fast, Viv could barely keep up.

What?! Did he just stop the laser with his mind?

Megdar let out a long sigh and clicked his tongue in disappointment. "So, this is the way you treat your *guests*, huh?" he hissed.

Megdar clenched his hand into a fist, crushing the laser blast into a fine dust.

He turned his attention toward Mr. Frank, the man who had the guts—or stupidity—to shoot at him. Charlotte reached out for her father, seeing the dangerous gleam in Megdar's eyes, but it was too late.

Megdar enveloped Mr. Frank in a force field of green light and lifted him ten feet in the air. Mr. Frank tried desperately to shake himself free, but the alien's power was too strong. Megdar closed his fist, dropping Mr. Frank to the floor with a thud, knocking him unconscious.

"Now you've made me angry."

Megdar puffed out his chest and pulled his arms back. His entire body began to shake. The glowing green in his eyes exploded out into two long rays of light. In a spreading wave, the same eerie green aura engulfed the entire army of aliens behind him.

Before Viv's eyes, the horde of Roswellians transformed into horrific creatures, worse than anything her nightmares could ever conjure up.

Their human arms and legs morphed into massive tentacles, each with thousands of tiny eyes that blinked in unison. On top of their heads, a long row of bright black spikes extended down their backs. Their massive green torsos hovered above wisps of smoke that rotated beneath them like ghostly helicopter blades. They looked like a terrifying mash-up of a squid, a centipede, and a spider. But if all those creatures had come from another planet.

"FIRE!" Director Harlow shouted from the center of the room.

Within seconds, a full-on war broke out in the main hall. Parents—or, Viv supposed, *agents*—unleashed their weapons from all angles. Bursts of light and electricity flew through the room. The massive aliens levitated together, gliding through the air like hot knives through butter. The entire room began to rumble, concrete and glass shattering in every direction.

Viv and her friends ducked for cover beneath a row of desks along the wall. It was utter chaos. Viv couldn't tell if her mind or her breathing was racing faster, and she could barely believe that just moments before, her biggest worry had been about making it to the lake.

The aliens emitted glowing force fields strong enough to knock their opponents to the floor in one easy motion. One after another, the agents were overpowered by the horde of monsters.

Viv watched through a crack in the desk as the aliens piled the unconscious adults in a heap to the side of the room. Both Charlotte's parents and Elijah's dad lay stunned and motionless in a deep sleep . . . At least she *hoped* they were just asleep . . .

But something even more sinister was happening in the opposite corner of the hall. The other employees' kids weren't quite as lucky as Viv and her friends hiding beneath the desk. One by one, as they were swept up and captured in the aliens' telekinetic grip, each kid was inspected by the monstrous creature who'd caught them before being placed into another pile.

What are they doing?

She raised her head above the desk and scanned the room for her mom. No sign of her. Though it was hard to see through the thick field of smoke that was filling the air.

Where is she?

Viv ducked back under the desk just as an alien shot a green wave of force field toward their corner of the room. It impacted the next desk over and sent it flipping through the air.

Peeking underneath the desk into the chaos, Viv realized Ray and Charlotte were gone, too. Her heart clenched in her chest.

I'm alone.

Her lungs were close to bursting from the effort of pushing down screams, which was all she wanted to do at this point. But she knew she had to stay quiet. Stay hidden. Stay safe.

Just like Mom said.

She peered around one of the desk legs and back out toward the battlefield.

The remaining employees of Area 51 were fighting their hardest, but it wasn't going to be enough. The Roswellians and their green energy beams were too strong. It wouldn't be long until they cleared everyone out of the middle of the room and made their way to those hiding in the back.

A hard yank pulled Viv out from under the desk. Her eyes snapped up to whatever had a hold of her ankle.

Mom!

"KEEP GOING! DON'T LOOK BACK!"

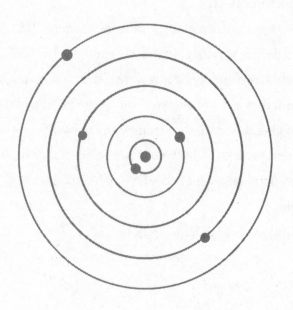

CHAPTER SIX

Viv's mind went blank for one terrifying moment. Her mother pushing her into the air vent, then seeing her ripped away by the aliens, and hearing the frightened gasps of Charlotte and Ray behind her were too much. It was all too much. But with her mother gone, nothing stood between the Roswellian army and the air vent where the three kids were hiding.

Viv had to think fast. She scrambled back toward the air vent gate, intending to pull it closed before the aliens noticed that she and her friends were inside. But the gate was open too wide for her to reach the metal ring handle, no matter how much she stretched.

Come on! Just a little farther!

She reached out again, this time not noticing that the entire hall had grown eerily quiet.

The aliens turned in unison to face the vent. Viv's hiding place was no longer a secret. It would be only moments before they captured her and her friends, too.

Desperate, Viv reached with all her might toward the ring. All of a sudden, the gate began to rattle, seemingly on its own. Her gaze darted from the trembling ring to the wave of aliens rushing straight toward her. She squeezed her eyes shut, her fingers centimeters away from the ring, praying the gate would close.

Then . . .

BOOM!

The metal gate snapped shut. The noise from the main hall cut out in an instant. Viv, Charlotte, and Ray were plunged into silent darkness.

"Ray, go!" Viv shouted. "Keep crawling!"

Ray, the furthest inside in the vent, was now the leader. His voice trembled as he sniffled through his stuffy nose. "Do I have to go first?"

"YES!" Viv and Charlotte yelled.

It was dark and cramped, and the three kids quickly crawled through the cold airshaft, hoping to escape. For a while, the only thing Viv could hear was the sound of her own heartbeat drumming in her ears. Her legs ached and her elbows began to blister from the seemingly endless crawling. Ten minutes passed. Then twenty. Then thirty. Where they were heading, Viv didn't know. But they were safe . . . for now.

She kept looking back over her shoulder. Nothing was chasing them in these cramped quarters. Viv took a moment to catch her breath, realizing how lucky they were to not have been captured.

The vent gate . . . it closed on its own. Even though I couldn't reach it . . . Did one of the aliens close it by mistake? Did I imagine it?

"Guys . . ." Charlotte's voice finally broke through the silence, and her pace slowed. Viv and Ray followed suit. "We need to stop for a second."

"Why?" Viv asked.

"Um, what do you mean *why*?" Charlotte nearly shrieked. "How about aliens are REAL and our parents have been working in a top secret lab with crazy laser weapons and weird creatures this WHOLE time? And now our parents have been taken hostage by those very same weird creatures, and we're stuck like sausages inside ceiling vents, which, by the way, seems very unsafe! THAT's why!"

Panting from exertion, Charlotte closed her eyes for one brief moment. "What are we gonna do?!"

She was right. They couldn't just keep crawling forever.

We have to do something.

"I'm not hearing any suggestions!" Charlotte yelled, her eyes flying open as the vent walls rattled from her cries.

"Shhh! Keep it down!" Ray hushed her. "The killer aliens might have supersonic hearing!"

"I don't care if they're listening," Charlotte whispered, as much as Charlotte Frank was capable of whispering. "*We* don't even know where we are, so how could they?"

"We should do what Director Harlow said," he replied. "And she said to keep going."

"What about your dad, Ray? Who even knows what happened to him? Those aliens could be *eating* him right now!"

"Not if they're vegans! Or pescatarians. Or gluten-free. Or lactose intolerant. Anyone know if people are made of either gluten or milk?"

"Enough!" Charlotte interjected. "We have to fight back. You agree with me, right, Viv?"

"Fight back?" Viv's mind had been going a mile a minute, but even she hadn't gotten that far in her thought process. "Do we look like Batman and Robin to you?"

"Hey! What about me?" Ray scoffed. "There's three of us here!"

"RAY! Shush!" Charlotte snapped. "We can be the Three Stooges for all I care, but what matters is we have to fight for our parents."

Viv just stared at Charlotte. She wished she could borrow Charlotte's confidence and swoop in to save the day, just like her mom had, but that thought was quickly replaced by the image of the towering creatures. Fighting back against all of them seemed impossible.

And even if we tried fighting back, how would we ever beat them?

Ray echoed her thoughts. "Our parents had guns and training; what do we have? I don't even remember what the aliens were called—didn't the leader, Megdar, say they were Orwellian?"

"He said *Roswellian*," Charlotte corrected him.

The name suddenly clicked into place in Viv's mind.

"Roswell! They must have come from the site in Roswell, New Mexico. I've read about a UFO that supposedly crash-landed there back in 1947." Viv had always had an interest in looking into alien sightings, even fake ones, after she realized the significance of where her mom worked. It seemed like it was finally coming in handy.

"Wait, 1947? So that means those aliens are, like, at least in their seventies. We can take 'em!" Charlotte argued.

"Or they could count their age in dog years," Ray replied. "Then they'd be eleven. That's a pretty fair fight—I can take an eleven-year-old."

"But still, they're way too powerful to fight head-on," Viv said quietly, staring down at her shoes. "If they can knock out all of our parents and the other Area 51 employees, there's probably not much the three of us can do on our own."

"Okay, Viv's right," Ray squeaked. "We should give ourselves up to the aliens. Seems like the only sensible thing to do."

"What? Are you insane, mate?" Charlotte shouted back, her anger making her accent pop out stronger. "I'm not gonna let those aliens fry me up as an arvo snack!"

"They don't EAT people, Charlotte! I thought we already established that they hate gluten. Besides, maybe they'll take pity on us if we turn ourselves in. Don't you think I look pretty pitiful?" Ray turned to Viv, Bambi eyes in full effect.

Viv looked into Ray's eyes, only to notice he was shaking. Underneath all his quips about food intolerances, he was just as scared as she was.

"H-hold on. Give me a second to think," Viv stuttered. Her head was spinning. She wished she knew what to do to save her friends and her parents, but instead all she could do was stare at her hands and hope for a plan to magically come to her.

"Wait!" Charlotte whispered, breaking Viv's concentration. "Do you hear that?"

Ray and Viv listened in silence. Nothing. But Viv knew Charlotte had an extra-keen sense of hearing, after training her ear for music to pick up even the smallest sounds and tone changes, so it didn't surprise her when Charlotte pushed her hair back and pressed the side of her face into the cold floor of the vent.

"I hear voices," Charlotte said after a moment. "Coming from below us."

Oh no. They found us.

"What do you hear? Who is it?"

Charlotte listened for a moment. Her face suddenly twisted into a frown. "It's Megdar. And someone else. Two voices."

Viv's stomach dropped. Even the sound of Megdar's name sent a shiver down her spine.

"Who's he talking to? Another alien?" Ray whispered.

"I don't know. I don't think so. The second voice . . . It

sounds so familiar. I can't quite place it."

"Well, can you hear what they're saying?"

Charlotte shot Ray an icy glare. "Maybe if you'd stop talking, I could!"

Ray clasped his hands over his mouth as Charlotte closed her eyes, smushed her ear against the floor, and focused.

"They're saying something . . . something about a key."

She listened in for another long moment. The fact that they were this close to Megdar made Viv's guts churn.

A key? What if it's the key to the vent? So they can find us?

"We should keep moving," Viv whispered. Charlotte nodded and prodded Ray forward.

Finally, after what felt like an hour more of silent crawling, they reached a spot where another vent shaft crossed theirs. Small beams illuminated the grates in the vent floor from the room below, the first hint of direct light they'd seen in a while.

Viv gripped the cold metal grate, peering down past her fingertips. She looked into the room below . . . and gasped.

Aha!

Through the grate, Viv could see a sprawling armory filled with high-tech guns, blasters, and futuristic ammunition. Rows upon rows of advanced-looking pistols, body suits, axes, whips, and what appeared to be flamethrowers lined the walls. She read a sign above the exit door below.

The Gadgets Room!

Mom must have sent us down this vent so we could find this room!

"Guys, look!" Viv tapped on the metal bars underneath her hands. Charlotte and Ray leaned out over the grate.

"Holy moly," Charlotte said with a grin.

"Let me see!" Ray exclaimed, clumsily shuffling closer for a better look.

As Ray squirmed his way between them, his elbow bumped into Charlotte's. Before anyone could react, Ray's glasses slid off the bridge of his nose and fell perfectly through one of the slits in the grate.

ZAP!

The glasses were instantly vaporized by a laser beam. They fizzled down to the floor of the Gadgets Room, reduced to ash. A stunned silence filled the vent.

"Those were brand-new glasses!" Ray cried out.

"Not anymore," Charlotte replied.

"Thankfully, I wear contacts, too."

"You wear glasses *and* contacts, Ray?"

"Yup. Just in case something like this happens. Plus, Dad says it gives me forty-forty vision, so it's twice as good!"

Viv carefully gazed down through the metal bars to assess what had just happened. She reasoned that the slightly smoking security device mounted on the wall of the armory must have had a motion sensor in order to blast the glasses to pieces. More red lights blinked along the ceiling. Meaning, more security blasters were ready to fire and vaporize them.

The tech and gadgets in that room were their only hope of saving their parents. Time was running out, and Viv needed to come up with a solution.

But right now, she knew only one thing for sure.

If any of us go down there, we're toast.

CHAPTER
SEVEN

"I see no other choice," Charlotte declared, after Viv explained her hunch about the blasters. "We've got to sacrifice Ray."

"Nuh-uh! No way!" Ray cried out.

"Well, then we're stuck here."

"Better to be stuck here than get turned into a fried churro!"

"You're already forty percent churro, Ray!"

"Forty percent churro, sixty percent awesome whiz-kid genius. You can't just throw all this away!"

As Charlotte and Ray continued to bicker about percentages, Viv tuned them out to focus.

Think, Viv. What would Mom do?

Viv knew her mom always preached about the importance of taking the time to assess a situation fully before making a move. She'd been on the other end of that well-meaning lecture one too many times, in fact, most recently after the last time she'd tried to convince her mom to let her have a pet penguin in Nevada. She looked back to the blaster that shot Ray's glasses. She noticed a tiny LED light on the front of the device was shut off.

Hmm . . . Could it be . . . ?

Viv's eyes traced the edges of the ceiling below them. She counted the laser blasters mounted on the walls. The other five lights still blinked red.

Maybe we can outsmart this thing . . .

"Guys! Look at that light." Viv pointed through the grate. "It turned off! You know what that means?"

"Somebody forgot to replace the batteries?" Ray asked.

"Batteries? We're at Area 51, Ray. You really think they use double As here?" Charlotte said.

"I think it means the blasters can only fire one laser each," Viv said, ignoring Charlotte. "Once it does, the light turns off, and it's basically powerless. It's like a can of Silly String that's empty after the first spray!"

"Silly String . . . of death!" Charlotte noted.

"You know what I mean. Maybe if we throw something big enough, it will trigger all the blasts at once, and then we'll be safe to drop down."

"Like I said. Ray!" Charlotte said, patting him on the shoulder. "Thanks for taking this one for the team."

"Ha ha. Very funny." Ray stuck his tongue out at Charlotte. "Just because I like churros doesn't mean I want to get fried up like one!"

ZAP!

Ray and Charlotte flinched as another blast fired below. They carefully turned around to see Viv smiling back at them, her right foot bare and her shoe in her hand.

"Viv! What did you do? Are you okay?" Ray whispered.

"My toes are a little cold. But hey, that sock was dirty anyways." Viv smirked. "Only four blasters left."

Dust sprinkled down to the floor. Another blaster's red light blinked off. Viv's sock had worked like a charm.

"Viv, you're one hundred percent brilliant!" Charlotte proclaimed.

The other two kids quickly followed her lead and searched for small objects to use against the motion detectors, any plans for dropping Ray down forgotten once they realized that small objects worked just as well against the motion detectors. Charlotte dropped a guitar pick she had in her pocket. Viv dropped the two extra hair ties that were wrapped around her wrist.

ZAP! ZAP! ZAP!

Three more lights blinked off . . . Only one remained. The two girls looked at Ray, who hadn't dropped anything yet.

"What? I'm sorry! I'm not wearing any socks!" Ray mewled.

"Well, you gotta throw *something*!" Charlotte said.

Without a second thought, Ray whipped off his jeans and shoved them through the grate. The particle blast vaporized the pants like the last crispy log in a bonfire.

"Oh geez, Ray! Really?!" Viv shielded her eyes.

"Aw, shoot!" Ray exclaimed. "The rest of my churro was in there!"

Viv caught sight of his underpants—a pair of giant boxer shorts with a racecar pattern.

"Nice undies, Ray!" Charlotte teased.

"Hey, laugh all you want! But they make me aerodynamic!"

With all the security devices deactivated, the kids safely dropped down from the air vent and onto a large titanium table before swinging their legs toward the floor. The lights in the room illuminated when their feet hit the paneled ground.

Whoa . . .

The walls were covered floor to ceiling with gadgets, weapons, and hardware the likes of which Viv had never seen before. There were what looked like heat-seeking missiles, explosive crossbows, and even a wall of brightly colored un-labeled potions that bubbled and glowed.

"Guys, before we do anything, we should be careful," Viv cautioned. "We don't know what any of this stuff does. This is probably all highly classified and dangerous equipment—"

"WOOOOOOO!" Charlotte howled, zooming by on a high-tech hoverboard. She effortlessly glided around the desks, pedestals, and wall-mounted equipment.

"Charlotte! Please be caref—"

"DON'T MOVE!" a voice cracked out from the back of the room.

A shiver shot up Viv's spine. Charlotte tumbled off the

hoverboard and headfirst into a box of unmarked shiny devices. Viv and Ray ducked beneath the table faster than the racecars on Ray's underwear.

"Show yourself!" the voice called. "I know you're in here!"

Oh no. It's them. It's the aliens. We're done for.

Viv peeked over the desk, hoping to get a glimpse of the alien's position.

A figure emerged from behind a glass tube positioned near the back wall. Covered in an orange mesh suit, the mysterious human figure held a box of Tic Tacs in his left hand like a weapon. Whoever it was, he couldn't have been more than a few inches taller than Viv. Certainly not an alien.

"I'm not afraid to use this thing!" the shaky voice called out.

Wait a second . . . That voice . . . I know that voice . . .

Viv took a deep breath, praying that she was right.

"*Elijah?*" she said through the quiet of the room.

The mint-wielding figure stopped. In one quick motion, he pulled down the mesh covering his face. Viv could see his tufts of jet-black hair and dark brown eyes.

It's him!

She jumped up from behind the desk.

"*Viv?*" Elijah said, a look of relief spreading across his face. "You made it out of there?"

Viv couldn't believe her eyes. The pounding in her heart from a few moments ago was still there . . . but for a totally different reason now.

"Thank goodness you're okay!" Elijah said, setting down the tiny box of mints and breathing out a massive sigh.

Thank goodness you're *okay.*

Charlotte wrenched her head out from the bucket of gizmos and looked toward Elijah. "Hey, mate, what were you thinking with the Tic Tacs? You're in a room full of weapons, and you grab *that*?"

"Yeah . . . I dunno," Elijah said sheepishly. "I grabbed the first thing I saw on the desk over there. In the dark, I thought maybe it was a grenade or something. I heard the rustling from the vent above and thought maybe you were aliens coming in here to get some more firepower. So I switched the security lasers back on and hid. And the next thing I knew, a sock fell out of the ceiling."

"Wait a second. How'd *you* get in here?" Charlotte asked.

"My dad . . . He saved me. Right when the aliens started to attack, he gave me the door code and told me how to find this place. He said to get in here and find this suit . . . so I took off running." Elijah looked toward the floor. "The last I saw of him, he, you know . . . got taken . . ."

The sadness in his voice was so overwhelming, Viv couldn't help but feel her throat clench up in response.

"Why did your dad tell you about that suit?" Charlotte asked. "What does it do?"

"I have no idea. But my dad said to find *this* suit specifically." Elijah turned around, showing off a large metal box attached to the back of the mesh.

"Wow! You look like a superhero!" Ray said, stepping forward to get a better look.

"Uh, thanks? Dude, where are your pants?"

"Dust in the wind, my friend," Ray replied. "Dust in the wind."

"Okay, guys, listen up," Viv said. "Let's look through everything, grab whatever might be helpful, and keep moving."

But she was too late. Charlotte was already back on the hoverboard, flying around the room like a little blond Tasmanian devil.

"Now, *she's* got the right idea!" Elijah gave Ray a playful nudge and ran off to grab his own piece of highly classified and dangerous equipment.

"Guys, seriously! We can't stay for very long!" Viv said.

"How are we supposed to fight off the aliens if we don't even know how to *use* this stuff!" Charlotte replied as she picked up a crossbow. "What even *is* all this?"

A large desk at the back of the room caught Viv's eye. She wandered over to it and picked up a shiny plaque that sat next to a World's Best Dad mug.

"Charlotte . . . look!"

Charlotte zoomed over, picked up the plaque, and examined it.

"Created by . . . *Desmond Frank*? Hey, that's my dad!" She grinned. "And that's the mug I gave him for his birthday!"

"Charlotte . . . I think this must be your dad's office!"

Charlotte's eyes lit up. "Wow . . . So this is his life's work? My dad's a genius! What other cool stuff does he have in here?"

Elijah and Charlotte were like kids in a candy shop. But in this case, the candy was awesome top secret, futuristic technology.

"Whoa, a freaking lightsaber!" Elijah shouted, pulling a hilt from a sheath marked "Lasersword."

Elijah gave it a test swing, extending a six-foot neon turquoise beam across the room. It slashed through the air. Everyone instinctually ducked, except for Ray, whose hair tips were instantly burned off.

"HEY! Watch the hair! This took me eleven years to grow!" Ray cried.

"You're only eleven years old, Ray!" Viv said.

"Exactly!" Ray said. "And I was bald as a baby, so imagine if I had to start back at square one!"

"Here we go, Ray! A new pair of glasses for you." Charlotte pulled sleek frames from a glowing case.

"Ooh! I like the design," Ray replied, taking the glasses from Charlotte and fixing them on his temples.

Ray's face dropped. He ripped the glasses off, threw them on the counter, and backed away slowly.

"What is it? What'd you see, Ray?" Viv asked.

"I—uh—I just saw all of your skeletons," he whimpered.

"X-ray glasses? That's awesome!" Elijah picked up the frames and put them on. He examined everyone up and down.

"Charlotte, looks like you have a hairline fracture on your pinky toe," Elijah reported.

"I KNEW it! Told you!" Viv boasted. "You gotta stop playing guitar with your feet!"

Charlotte laughed before approaching a large steel tube with sliding doors. "I wonder what's behind here . . ." She randomly pressed buttons on the wall.

CLICK!

Everyone gasped. The sliding steel walls of the tube cracked apart and slowly opened.

Inside was a suit of armor: deep purple and glowing with magenta veins of electricity. Elijah dropped the X-ray glasses in awe. Viv approached the tube.

"*Wow*," they both said at the same time.

Along the side of the tube, an engraved sign read "Combat Suit."

"That thing looks awesome! I think it might fit you, Viv," Elijah said, encouragement radiating out of his broad smile.

Viv could feel her stomach tie up in knots.

"Really? You think so?" Viv ducked her head to keep him from seeing her blush.

The purple combat suit was like something Tony Stark would build. She stepped up onto the platform and stuck her legs in before zipping up the front with one pull. The armored metal on the outside made the suit heavy, but it fit her like a glove.

A chirp rang out on Elijah's suit.

"Huh? What was that sound from?" Elijah asked, fiddling with the buttons on his wrist.

Instantly, Viv's body suit lit up. A tiny holographic Elijah projected up from the screen on her own wrist.

"Hey!" Viv exclaimed. "I can see you, Elijah!"

"Whoa! Looks like those two suits have wrist communicators!" Ray said, amazed at the tiny projection of Elijah.

Viv's heart skipped a beat.

Even our suits are linked up . . .

A loud clack came from Elijah's back as he continued to fiddle with the buttons. In one swift motion, two huge expandable orange wings snapped out of the metal box on his back. A jetpack-like engine descended beneath each wing.

"WHOA!" Elijah shouted.

"Holy cow! Elijah, it's a flight suit!" Charlotte exclaimed.

Elijah laughed. "Of course! I shoulda known that Dad would point me to the suit with wings!"

"That's so cool!" Viv said. The thought of seeing Elijah soaring through the sky made her weak in the knees.

Wow. He really is a superhero.

"Ray! Come over here. You gotta check this stuff out!" Charlotte said.

"Uh, thanks, but no thanks. I prefer to peruse from a safe distance," he said nervously. "I'm a browser, not a buyer."

"Oh yeah? Or maybe you're just too scared to try any weapons," Charlotte teased.

"Yeah, Ray. Pick something up!" Elijah said. "You don't want to face those aliens empty-handed. Especially without pants."

Ray instinctively crossed his legs. "Uh, I don't know . . . Everything in here seems like it will end up hurting me," he mumbled. "What about this thing? It looks pretty cool!"

He picked up a pen sitting by some blueprints on the workbench.

"Ray . . . I think that's just a normal pen," Viv said.

"Yeah, but look at how nice the ink is. Definitely fine point. This could definitely come in handy," Ray declared, slipping the pen into his shirt pocket.

"Here, how about this, Ray?" Elijah asked, retracting the wings of his suit back into their holsters and picking up a dark blue, pocket-size gun that had block lettering etched into the side: "Growth Ray." "See? It's even got Ray in the name!"

"Looks simple enough," Ray mumbled.

"Wanna try it out now?" Viv asked.

"No, I'm okay . . ." Ray cautiously took the growth ray from Elijah and gingerly tucked it into his shirt pocket. "I'm sure I'll figure it out when I need it."

"It's perfect for you. You'll finally be the tallest guy in school!" Charlotte laughed.

"Hey! I'm not short! I'm just small-boned."

Viv looked down at the purple suit that fit her body like a glove. She felt *powerful*. And that power was a comfort after feeling entirely too vulnerable in the wake of the alien attack. She moved her hand around inside of the arm cannon. Her fingers felt something. A trigger. Viv adjusted her grip to get a better feel.

BOOM!

A huge purple energy blast shot out from her palm, and there was an earsplitting eruption—it had destroyed the hoverboard Charlotte left on the floor.

"Crikey!" Charlotte shouted. "I wanted to keep that!"

Viv clenched her teeth. The explosion was loud. Too loud. Anyone nearby could've heard that blast.

Uh-oh.

Just then, a massive shadow floated by the door leading to the hallway. All four kids ducked for cover. Two more shadows stopped in front of the frosted glass entrance to the armory.

Viv cupped her hand over her mouth to quiet her breathing. She could almost make out a distorted conversation from the corridor.

It's them.

The Roswellians are right outside the door.

CHAPTER
EIGHT

Viv cautiously pressed her ear to the wall to listen in on the aliens' conversation. Charlotte and Elijah stood on guard by the door. Ray hid behind the counter, the growth ray trembling in his sweaty palms.

The sound was muffled, but Viv could make out a few words.

"You two! What are you imbeciles doing?" the voice boomed through the wall.

Viv recognized that voice.

Megdar. The alien leader.

Viv gritted her teeth, thinking of the way this evil monster had attacked her mother.

"We thought we heard something, Megdar," one of the other alien voices chimed in, raspy and low.

"You should be looking for the key! How did you two lose the key?"

"Sorry, boss! It can be tough holding on to it with these

tentacles," one of the underlings replied. "But first, we just thought we heard somethi—"

"You fools!" Megdar snapped, cutting off their warning. "Your only task was to find the progeny so we could leave this planet. And where did you get those churros? Spit them out!"

There was a pause, and then Viv heard the soggy splat of what must have been two semi-chewed churros hitting the tile floor.

"Now we have to find both the progeny *and* the key!" Megdar continued. "Go! Go! Find them NOW!"

"Yes, sir!"

The three shadows floated beyond the door's threshold and out of sight.

As Megdar's shadow floated away down the hallway, Viv heard him whisper to himself, "Can't believe they didn't get me a churro, too . . ."

And with that, things were quiet once again. The kids waited in silence for a moment. Perhaps it was a trap and the aliens had known they were hiding out in the Gadgets Room all along. Or perhaps they were safe.

Viv motioned to her friends to stay still before pointing toward the room's exit. Elijah nodded in agreement. Charlotte grabbed a random item out of a nearby bin, a pair of bronze gauntlets, and slipped them onto her hands. Ray let out a nervous squeaker of a fart from behind the workbench. A bead of sweat rolled down Viv's forehead.

Viv held up her fingers, silently counting down.

Three . . . two . . .

"One!" she whispered.

She slammed her palm on the door's Exit button, opening the doors to the hallway. Elijah and Charlotte burst out into the corridor. They stood back-to-back, aiming in opposite directions, as if they were a pair of well-trained soldiers, ready to take on the aliens. But no sounds or blasts rang out.

"Coast is clear, Viv," Charlotte reported, looking down at the mysterious new gloves on her hands.

"AHHHH!"

Ray wildly stumbled out of the Gadgets Room with his growth ray held straight up in the air, pen stuck on his shirt pocket. Without pants, he didn't look like much of a threat.

"Shhh!" Charlotte clapped her hand over Ray's mouth. "Do you want them to come back?"

Ray lowered his arms and straightened his shirt with a huff.

"And good job farting while we were trying to stay quiet." Charlotte smacked Ray on the back of the head, her annoyance mixing with clear relief that they were safe for now.

"Ow! I'm sorry! You KNOW I get gassy when I'm nervous!"

"And when you're not nervous."

"True, true."

"And honestly, with just that dinky little growth ray, I don't know how much help you'll be. Here, take these, too."

Charlotte shoved a pouch into his chest.

"Wh-what are these?" Ray asked.

"I dunno. I just grabbed 'em."

Viv leaned over and read the label on the pouch.

Sonic Grenades?

Ray reached in and delicately pulled out the slip of paper inside.

"Charlotte! This says that when you detonate one, 'they're so loud that they rip a hole in the space-time continuum and teleport objects through unknown wormholes'!"

"Yada yada, blah blah. Science stuff. Just keep them. You never know when you might need a grenade!" Charlotte said, a gleeful glint in her eye.

"Uhh, I don't know . . . I kinda like to keep space and time as . . . continuous . . . as possible," Ray said.

"Viv, could you hear what the aliens were talking about?" Elijah asked.

"Yeah," she said, "they were talking about a lost key and . . . 'the progeny'?"

"Oh right," Elijah replied. "Didn't Megdar say he was after 'the progeny' back in the main hall?"

"What does that even mean?" Charlotte asked.

"*Progeny* means 'offspring,'" Viv said.

"Off spring?" Charlotte said. "So, like, autumn?"

"No." Viv sighed. "*Offspring* meaning 'child.'"

"Like an alien child?"

"Guys?" Ray called out, leaning up against a corner in the hallway. He reached down into a stainless steel drain on the floor and pulled out something wedged between the metal bars. "Looks like the aliens left something behind," he whispered.

Ray slowly lifted his balled-up fist. Everyone crowded around his hand.

He uncurled his fingers and held up a tiny green sphere.

"What is that?" Charlotte asked.

The speckles on the outside of the orb looked strange. Almost familiar . . .

Uh-oh.

"Is that . . ."

The little orb in Ray's hand started to shake and wiggle.

"It's . . . it's . . . ," Viv stuttered.

"An egg!" Ray shouted, finishing her sentence.

"And it's hatching!"

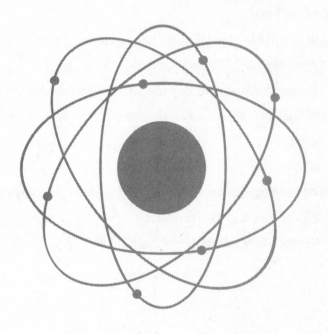

CHAPTER NINE

A tiny green foot cracked through the eggshell in Ray's hand.

Elijah and Charlotte jumped back. Viv aimed her arm cannon at the alien, convinced that a smaller version of the monstrous Megdar was about to hatch. Viv's memory flashed back to what that evil beast did to her mother. She wouldn't let the same thing happen to her friends.

"NO! Don't shoot!" Ray cried. "I need all my fingers! Toes, too!"

Another green foot broke through the shell.

"What do I do? What do I do?!" Ray squirmed. "I'm not ready to have a kid!"

"Don't move a muscle!" Viv instructed. "We don't know what that thing could do."

Ray shut his eyes tightly. He held his breath, trying to stay as still as possible as the small alien life awoke in his palm.

The egg split down the middle and peeled to either side. Viv charged an energy beam, ready to obliterate whatever emerged. Even if it was just a freaky alien chicken.

But the creature that popped out of the egg was nothing like the giant Roswellians. Or a creepy chicken. In fact, the infant alien was like nothing the four kids had ever seen before.

Two big floppy ears framed a green fuzzy face. Four little legs squirmed under its apple-shaped body, and a small antenna stuck out of its head right above three adorable puppy-dog eyes. It was the size of a ripe kiwi. With all the strength the little alien could muster, it picked up its head and purred lovingly into Ray's palm.

Viv's, Elijah's, and Charlotte's jaws dropped. For a moment, they were speechless.

"Okay, that thing is straight-up adorable," Viv cooed as she lowered her arm cannon to her side.

"Meekee!" the tiny alien peeped.

Ray quietly sobbed with his eyes still clenched tight. His knees wobbled and sweat dripped from his hairline.

"Meekee!" The little creature peered up at Ray with love in its eyes.

"Ray?" Viv said.

"Yes?" he squeaked back, still terrified.

"You can put it down now. I don't think that thing's gonna hurt you."

Ray squirmed and placed the baby alien down on the floor before backing away in a panic.

"Meekee! Meekee!" the alien cried out.

"Meekee?" Elijah knelt down to inspect the alien closer. "I guess that's your name, huh, little guy?"

Ray hid behind a concrete column. Meekee waddled over on his little legs to get closer to him.

"Aw! I think he likes you, Ray!" Viv grinned.

"Ray, he thinks you're his mommy!" Elijah chimed in.

"No!" Ray shouted. The tiny alien followed Ray with every step, a newborn duckling trailing its much larger mama.

"Get away from me!" Ray ran around in circles trying to shake his new little shadow. "I'm not ready to be a mom! I'm an aunt at best!"

After a few laps, Meekee got dizzy and fell over, letting out a cute giggle and then the tiniest burp.

"I don't know, Ray." Elijah laughed. "Looks like he inherited your gassy gene!"

"Cute or not, he's with the enemy," Charlotte interjected. She scooped Meekee up into her hand. "Listen here, little guy, do you know where our parents are?"

"Charlotte, I don't think you're going to get much information out of him," Viv said.

"He knows something, I can tell!"

"Meekee!" the baby alien chirped in response.

"Seems like he doesn't have the widest vocabulary," Elijah said.

"It's just a baby, Char," Viv added.

"A baby monster!" Charlotte said, pointing an angry finger

at a wide-eyed Meekee. The little alien stuck out a pink little tongue and gave her finger a lick like she was an angry Australian lollipop.

Viv looked at the baby creature and realized . . .

"Wait a second," Viv said. "What if *this* is the progeny?"

"You think this little guy is what Megdar is looking for?" Elijah asked.

"It makes sense."

"Why would your mom steal him from Megdar?" Charlotte asked.

"Maybe she's starting her own line of alien Beanie Babies?" Ray offered.

"Although," Elijah said, ignoring Ray's comment, "why would the aliens leave him behind so carelessly?"

"I don't know. Maybe they lost track of him during the battle," Viv replied. "Maybe if we give Meekee back to the aliens, there's a chance they'll leave this planet in peace."

"Meekee?" The alien chirped up again at the sound of his name.

"That's enough out of you," Charlotte snapped, putting Meekee onto the ground.

The hatchling tried to climb Charlotte's leg to be held once again, but Charlotte recoiled in disgust. Meekee scrunched up his face into a grimace. Tears started to well in his three big, almond-shaped eyes.

"MEEKEE! Meekee! Meekee!" the teeny alien cried out.

"Charlotte! Look what you did!" Ray shouted over Meekee's squealing.

"What *I* did? You're his mom! You handle this, Ray!" Charlotte said.

"MEEKEE! MEEKEE!"

Everyone looked to Ray.

"Don't look at me! I told you I'm barely an aunt!"

"MEEKEE! MEEKEE! MEEKEE! MEEKEE!"

"Maybe he needs to poop!" Ray shouted. "I cry when I have to poop, too."

"TMI, Ray!"

Meekee's cry suddenly morphed into a high-pitched alarm, a sound that seemed much too loud to be coming out of such a tiny body.

The four kids covered their ears as Meekee's siren-like cry pierced the air. Viv felt the ground begin to vibrate under her feet.

This is not good.

"MEEKEE! MEEKEE! MEEKEE!" the baby wailed.

"Make him stop!" Charlotte shouted.

Ray reluctantly scooped Meekee up into his hands and gave him a loving pat on the head.

"There, there, little weird alien freak. It's okay. Aunt Mommy is here!" Ray soothed.

But it was too late. Viv realized what was happening.

Meekee's alerting the other aliens. They're coming for us.

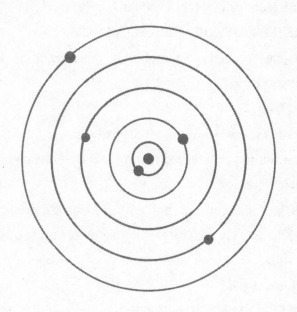

CHAPTER
TEN

The entire hallway shook like an earthquake was rumbling the floor. Viv rushed over and peeked around the corner. She was right. *They* were coming.

Two fully grown Roswellian aliens sped directly toward the four of them. Each of them glowed that sick, bright green color that made Viv's skin crawl. Their tentacles flailed in spirals as they zoomed closer to the huddle of friends.

Viv quickly did the math in her head. Two aliens versus four kids armed to the teeth. The enemy was outnumbered.

We . . . might actually have a chance.

The alien beasts zoomed along side by side until they diverged fifty yards from the corridor where the kids stood. Viv's heart skipped a beat.

Behind them, Megdar appeared, looming larger and faster than the other two Roswellian soldiers in his alien form.

Viv felt her blood boil at the sight of him. She held down the trigger in her arm cannon, filling the blaster with a full burst. Her arm buzzed with its intense power. The aliens were closing in, now only a few yards away.

"STOP!" Viv screamed. She fired the purple energy blast up into the air just above the aliens' heads. Concrete rained down from the ceiling where it hit.

It worked. The three Roswellians stopped dead in their tracks. Elijah, brave as ever, stepped forward from behind Viv.

"Don't attack! We know why you're here!" Elijah shouted.

He nudged Ray, urging his nervous friend to present Meekee on cue.

Megdar emerged from behind his two subordinates, peering down at the four defiant kids. A look of bewilderment filled his thousands of beady eyes.

With each precious second ticking by, Elijah snapped his head toward Ray.

"Ray!" he angrily whispered. "Give him the baby!"

Ray patted the place where his jean pockets would have been, if he had been wearing pants. He spun around in a tight circle, searching for the tiny alien who had been crying next to him just a moment before.

"Um . . . I think he's gone!"

"He's gone? What do you mean he's gone?"

"Baby went bye-bye, Elijah. That's what I mean!" Ray said, his naked knees trembling beneath him.

The aliens on either side of Megdar glowed neon green, ready to pounce on the infuriating children who dared to stand in the way of their leader's plans.

"Wait! I swear, he was just here!" Elijah yelled. "We have what you want!"

Megdar advanced toward the kids. He loomed over them, nearly blocking out all of the light from the fluorescents above.

"Yes . . ." Megdar's voice boomed menacingly. He stared down at Viv, as if he was peering through her soul.

"You do."

Viv felt like a fly under his horrible microscope. Megdar lifted his tentacles and commanded his underlings.

"Subdue these children. But don't harm the progeny."

And with that final word, the Roswellian underlings lunged toward them.

Elijah extended the wings on his flight suit and leapt up from the floor. A trail of vapor followed his path as he soared through the hallway. Viv fired a round of blasts from her arm cannon at the Roswellians. The aliens quickly dodged them both and descended down low, straight toward Ray and Charlotte on the floor.

"Charlotte . . . I sure hope those gloves are more than just a cute accessory!" Ray cried out. "DO SOMETHING!"

"Okay, let's see what these bad boys can do!" Charlotte said, clenching her fists and closing her eyes. The gauntlets on her hands glowed with bright neon light. Around her, an army of Charlotte clones materialized out of thin air.

Fifty identical Charlottes!

"WHOA!" the dozens of fake Charlottes, or Farlottes, yelled in unison. Viv couldn't believe her eyes. Mr. Frank had created these? He really was a genius.

The original Charlotte smiled and thrust her arm forward. "YES! Good on ya, mates!" she said as she commanded her fifty clones to attack.

The Farlottes climbed onto one of Megdar's underlings, wrestling each of its tentacles. But the alien fought back, using its telekinetic abilities to fling the clones off its thrashing body one by one.

Viv fired another shot, but the blast exploded just short, accidentally disintegrating four of the Farlottes in an instant.

"Sorry, Charlotte!" Viv called out.

"No worries, mate! Didn't feel a thing!" the now hundreds of clones yelled in unison.

Viv re-aimed her arm cannon, this time hitting the alien dead-on. The Roswellian deflated instantly, flying backward out toward the hallway exit.

One down. Two more to go.

Purple smoke floated through the air with each blast from Viv's cannon. The smell of jet fuel from Elijah's flight suit filled Viv's nostrils as he soared through the air, using his wings as a battering ram against the dozens of tentacles flailing around the ceiling. Charlotte's clones flew around the hall in a frenzy, grabbing at each alien appendage and pulling the remaining Roswellian soldier toward the ground. But it still wasn't enough.

Ray quivered against the wall, trying not to be hit by falling debris.

"Hey, RAY! Now would be a good time to become the tallest guy in school!" Viv yelled over her shoulder.

Out of the corner of her eye, Viv watched as Ray desperately pawed at the buttons on his growth ray, his hands so sweaty that the ray kept slipping around in his hands. His hands were shaking so bad that it was nearly impossible for him to read the tiny control knob on the side of the pistol.

"RAY!" Viv snapped.

"I'm trying!" Ray fumbled with the gun, nearly dropping it before managing to point the ray at himself. Viv watched as he closed his eyes and finally held down the trigger.

A pulse of blue electricity passed over his skin.

Viv rattled off another shot at the remaining Roswellian soldier as Megdar hovered in the corner. She glanced back to where Ray had been moments ago.

But he was gone.

"Ray? Ray?! What happened?!" Viv shouted.

She watched as one of Charlotte's clones stomped by a tiny form on the floor, before the smallest pipsqueak of a voice came from it.

"I accidentally set the gun to *Shrink* mode!" Ray squealed.

Viv squinted down toward the floor. Ray was right. With one zap, he'd turned himself into the size of a ladybug.

He hadn't gotten bigger—he'd gotten way, way *smaller*.

Dang it! Wrong button, Ray!

Viv fired off another purple blast and turned back to her itty-bitty friend. The battle must've looked massive from his perspective.

He was already scared before . . . He must be terrified now!

But before she could help him, Viv watched as Ray's foot slipped between the metal bars of the grate on the floor he had been standing on. His teeny-tiny body dropped down through the crack. She could barely make out his scream as he plunged into darkness.

"Ray! NO!" Viv called out.

The remaining Roswellian underling hovered along the ceiling toward her. Viv tried to knock it down, but her energy blasts only found the concrete above. This one was faster than the other.

"I can't get a good shot from the ground!" Viv called out to the human tower of Charlotte clones desperately pushing back against Megdar's force fields.

Just then, Viv felt something snake under her arms. She twisted around, ready to blow away whatever had her in its clutches—but she stopped.

It was Elijah.

He lifted her up into the air with him, squeezing her tightly as they glided above the ocean of Charlottes below.

Oh my gosh. Oh my gosh. I'm in Elijah's arms!

From Viv's vantage point, he looked just like Superman. It

was the first time they'd ever been this close. His eyes glanced down toward hers, and Viv's heart pounded in her chest.

Boy, this would make a great first kiss.

"HEY! You ugly dingbats!" Charlotte shouted toward the aliens. "Why don't you pick on someone your own size when there's ten of 'em stacked on top of each other?"

Viv snapped out of her romantic daydream and back into reality. Charlotte had never been the best at trash talk, but still, she beckoned toward Megdar and his underling as they swooped down from the ceiling.

Bringing her hands together in one huge clap, Charlotte sent a wall of new clones flying toward the creatures. But the duplicates were no match for Megdar. With one whip of his tentacle, he turned them all into dust.

Viv saw her opportunity to strike. "Now!" she said to Elijah. He cut his wings hard to the right and propelled the two of them up through the wedge between Megdar and his underling. They soared through the air as Viv fired blast after purple blast from her combat suit, striking the underling with three direct hits. The Roswellian, beat up and exhausted, zoomed back toward the hallway's exit. Together, Elijah and Viv were unstoppable.

"Way to go, Viv!" Elijah smiled down at her. She felt a fluttering sensation in her gut. And not just because it was her first time flying with a jetpack!

"Where are you going?" Megdar roared at his retreating underlings. With them gone, Megdar was finally alone.

Viv knew this was their chance to take him down.

"Circle around! Get me closer!" Viv directed Elijah. He jutted to the left and cranked the engine on the flight suit to full power.

Viv locked in on her target and took aim, loading up a massive blast within her arm cannon while Megdar's back was turned. She was just about to pull the trigger when—

Megdar whipped around. The thousands of eyes across his head blazed with rage . . . directly toward Elijah.

An abrupt jerk ripped Viv out of Elijah's arms.

Within an instant, she felt gravity yanking her toward the floor. She was falling! Viv looked up to see Elijah, frozen in midair, wrapped in the terrible green glow of Megdar's telekinetic grip.

As Viv plummeted, time seemed to slow down. She stared up as she fell, seeing Elijah's body twisting in pain under Megdar's control.

She crashed into the ground with a bang, grateful that the metal shielding on her combat suit absorbed most of the impact.

Megdar laughed as Elijah struggled to break free from the alien's clutches.

NO!

Viv swelled with fury. First her mom, now Elijah. This monster would stop at nothing to hurt the people that mattered most to her. But she wouldn't let him.

Viv aimed her palm at the monster and held down her arm cannon's trigger. But it only clicked and rattled.

Not now! Come on! Work, you dumb cannon!

It was no use. The trigger was busted. The fall must've been too much for the suit to handle. Viv felt tears flood into her eyes. She wiped her cheeks and looked up at the boy suspended in midair—the boy she desperately wanted to protect.

"Viv . . ." Elijah choked out her name as Megdar tightened his grip.

Viv clenched her fist. The anger inside of her was too much to contain. She lifted her arm cannon to the ceiling and screamed.

A colossal blast of bright green energy exploded from her palm. The shot sliced through the air and slammed into Megdar, narrowly clipping Elijah's torso. The alien leader rocketed backward and smashed into the wall. Elijah dropped fifteen feet in an instant.

No!

He was inches away from crashing when a burst of his jet fuel kicked in, suspending him above the ground for just long enough to make a gentler landing. He collapsed into a heap on the floor.

Dazed and confused, Megdar retreated back down the hallway like his underlings.

"This is not the end!" he bellowed.

The green trail of light faded away behind him as he accelerated down the corridor.

And with his sudden exit, the hallway was now silent.

"That's right! You better run, you naughty little wombats!" the Charlotte clones yelled in unison as each began evaporating one after the other.

Viv's lungs pounded in her chest, and she struggled to catch her breath. The combat suit that fit her so perfectly moments ago in the Gadgets Room now felt like it was squeezing her too tight.

Elijah coughed, still curled up into a ball on the ground. Viv's heart dropped. There he was, the boy she'd liked since third grade, weak from a battle that almost cost him his life. Viv ached, knowing that if she'd had the courage to target Megdar sooner, maybe Elijah wouldn't have gotten hurt.

She rushed over to his side as he lifted his head up. She looked him over for any cuts or bruises. He flashed her that million-dollar smile, albeit a weak one.

"Thank goodness you guys are all right," Elijah said. Viv breathed a sigh of relief. Even after a close encounter with a powerful evil alien, he still couldn't help but think of others before himself.

"Forget about us. Are *you* okay?"

Elijah sat up slowly and clutched his side—in the exact spot where Viv's energy had blast brushed him before it crashed into Megdar. A tiny hole had burned through Elijah's flight suit, revealing a patch of raw, pinkish skin underneath.

"Oh no!" Viv felt her stomach curl into a knot. "I didn't mean to hit you! I'm so sorry!"

"Sorry? You saved my life!" Elijah's big brown eyes stared into hers. "If it wasn't for you, I'd be a pancake right now!"

Viv tried to smile back at him, but she couldn't calm the sense of guilt that was building in the back of her mind.

Why did I fire that shot? So stupid! And reckless!

What if my aim was off a fraction of an inch more?

What if I'd accidentally hit Elijah instead of Megdar?

Viv realized that she'd never felt anger that strong before . . .

I felt out of control. I really could've hurt someone . . . I could've hurt Elijah.

Elijah frowned, noticing the worry sneaking into Viv's expression. "Honestly, Viv. I'm fine, I promise."

Viv carefully helped him up off the floor as he started to regain his balance.

"I'm more worried about this dented wing than anything." Elijah motioned over his left shoulder and showed the semi-crushed edge of the wing that had broken his fall.

Viv took a deep breath and composed herself. Between Elijah's dented wing and her busted arm cannon, there were too many things going on right now to lose focus. They were still in serious danger.

If Megdar and his goons come back now, they'll squeeze us into orange juice. And not the good kind, either. The kind with pulp. And we'd be the pulp. Gross.

Elijah looked around the room. "Wait, where's Ray?"

"The doofus accidentally shrunk himself and fell down through there," Viv replied, pointing to the small grate on the floor near the beat-up column. "I'm worried about him."

"Looks like a sewer grate."

"Charlotte, where do you think that thing leads?" Viv asked.

Viv turned around to face her friend. She glanced up at Charlotte, catching sight of her bright blue eyes.

Then Charlotte's body evaporated into dust.

"Charlotte? Charlotte!" Viv rushed over to the spot where her friend stood just a second ago, grasping at the air left behind.

"Viv . . ." Elijah said.

It must have been one of her clones from the battle.

Viv and Elijah looked at each other, realizing that they were alone.

The *real* Charlotte was missing.

CHAPTER ELEVEN

"AHHHHHH!" Ray's lungs hurt from screaming.

Hurtling down a sewage tube in complete darkness after accidentally shrinking himself was not his idea of fun.

He had been sliding for what felt like hours through miles of muddy sludge. A roller coaster made of slime? Ray hated roller coasters to begin with, so the slime was just an added bonus of misery. He tried to press his miniature hands to the walls to slow himself down with friction, but the walls were too slick to get a good grip.

It was in this moment that Ray wished he hadn't sacrificed his pants to the lasers. At this point, he could even feel mud caked into his belly button. He wondered if he would ever feel clean again.

Just when he thought things couldn't get any worse, he felt something moving around in his shirt pocket. Terrified that it might be some crazy ooze slug hitching a ride, he nervously peered down.

A miniature version of Meekee clung for dear life to the

nice ink pen Ray had grabbed from the Gadgets Room.

"AHHHHHH!" Ray shrieked at the sight of the adorable baby creature.

"Meekeeeeee!" the tiny alien screamed back.

They screamed at each other for a few moments until a light appeared at the end of the tunnel.

Finally! An end to this nightmare!

The faint glow grew closer and closer as Ray's tiny body plummeted farther and farther down the pipes.

Suddenly, the tube he was riding in dropped sharply. Ray and Meekee fell straight down.

THUNK!

Ray flew out of the tube and landed in something tight. He was suddenly wedged between rough cotton and a stiff leather plate.

What the— Where am I? And what's that stench?

Ray pinched his nose closed. The smell was awful, like a sweaty cabbage. And somehow worse than the mud he was just riding through. He pressed his hands out to feel his surroundings and suddenly realized . . .

He was in a shoe!

And someone's wearing it!

And that someone needs a prescription for athlete's foot.

Ewww.

A booming voice from above brought Ray's eyes upward. He looked up along the massive leg to see it was a man in a suit. From this angle, Ray couldn't see his face, just the side of his gigantic ear.

"I grabbed this from the Gadgets Room for you," the man said. "It's what we here on Earth call a 'disposable camera.' Thought you might like it. Snap some shots of Earth as we leave."

Ray craned his neck to look over at the other person in the room.

AH!

Floating just a few feet away, Megdar loomed like a giant. Ray cupped his hand over his mouth to keep from screaming.

"What is this piece of junk? And how am I supposed to hold that with these tentacles?" Megdar asked, his voice booming through the small room. "You'd be surprised how hard it is to adjust after being stuck in human form for so long."

Ray stayed as quiet as the bug-size boy that he was. His heart pounded in his chest. Meekee clung to the pen in his pocket, looking a lot like a green, three-eyed koala bear. Although to be fair, biology had never been Ray's best subject.

I'm too small. If I just stay quiet, maybe they won't notice me!

"Good point. Guess I didn't consider that . . ." the man said. He tucked the camera back into his pocket. "How close are we to leaving?"

"Leaving? We're not going anywhere without the progeny," Megdar replied. "You bring me that, and then we'll all escape on the ship."

"Yes, sir. Absolutely. I'm on it," the man said.

"Oh, and can you bring me one more thing?" Megdar asked.

"Name it," the man replied.

"A churro."

"I'll . . . see what I can do," the man replied.

"Great. Don't let me down. Especially with the whole churro thing."

"You got it." The man turned to leave the room. "Ugh, disgusting. Hold on, there's some mud in my shoe."

The man kicked out his leg.

AHHHH!

Ray suddenly felt the urge to puke. His body rattled around between the man's ankle and the shoe like a muddy pinball. The man reached his hand down and flicked the booger that was Ray out of the shoe and down towards another sewage drain.

Ray and Meekee flew through the air. Ray looked down, seeing another stretch of sewage tubes below.

"NO! NO! Not again!" his little squeaky voice shouted. They landed in the pipe with a plink and continued their muddy journey through the complex.

This time, Ray just crossed his arms, unamused.

"How much sewage could one place have? I mean, really. This is ridiculous!" Ray said out loud to no one in particular.

As they rounded another corner, a light shone in from up ahead. He could see the drop coming this time.

"HOLD ON!" he shouted, clutching Meekee tight in his shirt pocket.

SPLASH!

Ray plunged feetfirst into a bucket of dirty water. He clasped his hand over his mouth, trying not to breathe in any of the liquids that now surrounded him. He fiercely paddled upward and tried to find a bubble of oxygen. He refused to drown in a foot of water.

He finally surfaced, grabbing at the plastic rim of the bucket to hang on for dear life. The stress of the moment made Ray fart, and the tiniest fart bubble in the entire universe bubbled up to the surface of the water.

Ray finally yanked his torso up over the edge and took a huge gulp of air. Meekee popped out of his shirt pocket, coughing up some of the water.

After catching his breath, Ray scrunched up his face and rubbed at his eyes, which were stinging from the gross water that had gotten in. He gingerly pulled out his contacts, now too contaminated to put back in. They sat in his muddy palm like two sad pepperonis. He tried to survey the room around him, but his vision was too blurry and he could now only make out basic shapes from far away.

So much for forty-forty vision.

Then his heart dropped.

He wasn't alone.

In the far corner, a giant blurry blob sat at a messy desk, its back turned to the bucket where Ray and Meekee hid. Its massive arms moved back and forth, as if tinkering with something. From this distance, with his unaided eyes, Ray couldn't tell if this blob was a friend or foe.

Ray dropped backward into the bucket to hide. He floated on his back in the water while Meekee sat patiently on his chest.

The little alien stared at him with wide eyes, as if wondering, "What do we do now?"

"I'm working on it, little guy," Ray said. "We could really use my meatball catapult right about now."

Think, Ray. What would Viv do in this situation?

He hoisted himself back onto the edge of the bucket, examining the room for any weapons he could use against whatever intimidating beast sat in the corner. A row of giant mops hung above an old sink. Shelves full of spray bottles, jugs, and what looked like rolls of paper towels bordered the walls.

Then, just as his eyesight was finally starting to go back to normal, it clicked. The mops. The cleaning supplies. The buckets of dirty water. He suddenly realized where he was.

The janitor's closet!

And that giant blob must be . . .

"DAD?" Ray's pipsqueak voice barely echoed off the insides of the bucket.

Al Mond fell out of his chair. He whipped around with a cautious look and picked up a nearby plunger, wielding the rubber tool like a baseball bat, ready to strike at the source of the high-pitched noise.

Ray couldn't tell who was more scared—him or his dad.

"Dad, it's me!" Ray's tiny voice pleaded. "RAY!"

His father slowly approached the bucket.

"Who's there?" he called out, taking a few practice swings of the plunger to show he meant business. "And what have you done with my boy?"

"Down here!" Ray shouted. "I'm in the bucket!"

Mr. Mond leaned in closer, adjusting the thick glasses on his face. The prescription was so strong that his eyes looked the size of dinner plates. He squinted into the bucket, before finally recognizing his itsy-bitsy son.

"Ray? Is that really you?"

"Yes! It's me! I accidentally shrunk myself!" Ray explained.

He pulled out the growth ray that was still miraculously tucked into the waistband of his underwear.

"See?" Ray held up the tiny device for his dad to examine. "But I don't know how to change back!"

"Okay! Stay calm, son!" Mr. Mond replied. "Here's what I want you to do—adjust the knob to size four and then pull the trigger *precisely* halfway."

"Uh . . . what happens if I pull the trigger *more* than halfway?" Ray inquired.

"Mmm. You ever look through a microscope in biology class?"

"Yeah?"

"You'll be even tinier than that."

Ray's mouth dropped open. "What's even tinier than microscopic?"

"Well . . . technically, nanoscopic, but that's not the point!

The point is, just pull the trigger halfway, Ray. And be careful!"

Ray followed his dad's instructions exactly and felt the same zap of electricity. He closed his eyes as he felt his molecules grow back to their normal size. Now, instead of drowning, Ray's butt was stuck in the bucket.

Mr. Mond leaned down and scooped Ray up in his arms. His butt popped out with a loud snap.

"My boy!" Ray's dad cried, pulling him in close for an emotional, muddy hug. "I thought the aliens got you, too!"

He pushed back from the embrace and examined the layers of grime covering his son.

"Um . . . Ray? Where are your pants?" Mr. Mond asked suspiciously.

Ray frantically recounted his journey up until this point. Crawling through the air vents. Raiding the Gadgets Room. The terrifying battle in the hallway. The conversation he overheard in the shoe. His father listened intently to the story's twists and turns, his eyebrows furrowing intensely at the overheard Megdar conversation in particular.

"Ray, that makes it sound like someone in Area 51 is conspiring with the aliens. Are you sure you were stuck in a human's sock and not one of the Roswellians'?"

"Well, I guess it could have been an alien sock . . . but I've smelled enough feet in my life to know it was human."

"How many feet have you smelled, Ray?"

"Enough."

Both Monds stared at each other for a long beat before moving on.

"Dad, there's something I don't understand," Ray wondered aloud. "How did *you* escape from the aliens when all the other adults were captured?"

"Well . . . uh, actually . . . I was in the bathroom. All that talk about space and coconuts had me feeling a little backed up," Mr. Mond said sheepishly. "When I finished up, I could tell trouble was brewing outside the door, so I did what anyone would do. I hid behind the toilet until the aliens left. I told you being short would someday save my life!"

Mr. Mond let out a half-hearted laugh, while Ray just eyed him with confusion.

"But you left all of your friends and coworkers behind," Ray said slowly. "And then they were all taken captive."

"Hey, all of the other employees had laser guns!" Mr. Mond defended himself. "What was I supposed to do? Spray the aliens with Windex?"

Ray and his father sat in silence for a moment while Ray thought back to the chaos he experienced in the battle outside the Gadgets Room. He didn't understand at the time how Viv, Elijah, and Charlotte were so brave.

But now, listening to his father, for the first time in his life, he understood.

They weren't brave for themselves . . . They were brave for one another.

Ray felt a wave of courage he had never felt before. When he needed them, his friends were always there. So why couldn't he be there for them?

Meekee sharply chirped out of Ray's pocket. He'd also returned to his normal kiwi-like size. The alien stuck his head above the pocket's edge and gave Ray's dad a sweet smile.

Mr. Mond jumped backward and knocked over an entire row of mops.

"Whoa!" he yelled. "What is *that* thing?" He grabbed the plunger again, ready to fend off the tiny alien life-form if need be.

Ray, terrified of the little creature just moments ago, calmly patted him on the head. "Dad, this is Meekee. We think he might be 'the progeny' the aliens are after. If we give Meekee back to the Roswellians, we might have a chance to save everybody!"

"You want to face the aliens? With no pants and a growth ray you don't even know how to use?" Mr. Mond asked. "What's gotten into you, Raymond? That sounds way too dangerous!"

"Well, it wasn't so dangerous when I had my friends with me," Ray said. "Do you have a better plan, Dad?"

"What do you think I've been doing here this whole time? Playing with brooms?" Mr. Mond asked. "Listen, son. I might not have access to all the same high-tech gadgets and technology as the other employees here, but that doesn't mean I'm useless. Where do you think you got that big scientific brain of yours?"

His dad motioned him over to a workbench draped with a stained linen tablecloth.

"Behold!" he bellowed proudly. "The one weapon that can defeat those aliens!"

He whipped back the linen sheet, revealing his magnum opus.

On the table sat a large dark brown gun that appeared to be made out of superglue and craft supplies. The barrel was twisted and misaligned, with screws popping out every which way. It looked like the world's worst kindergarten science project.

"Built it all by myself!" Mr. Mond bragged.

The side of the barrel had a chicken-scratch inscription clearly written in Sharpie: *O.D.O.R. Olfactory Deterrent Offensive Rifle.*

It took Ray a few seconds to realize what he was looking at . . .

"Um, Dad?"

"Pretty cool, huh?" Mr. Mond beamed.

"You built a fart gun?"

"Hey! It's not a *fart* gun! It's a sophisticated aromatic weapon!" His dad grunted. "It emits a cloud of potent, highly concentrated green gas that disorients even the largest enemies."

"Right. So . . . it's a fart gun."

"It's not!"

"Then show me how it works."

"Well, I can't do that. Detonating the O.D.O.R. in here? In such a small, enclosed room? We'd both get knocked out. Trust me, I've made that mistake before," Mr. Mond recalled with a haunted look in his eyes.

"Your plan is to hit the aliens with a stink blast?"

"Son, that's my plan with everything. How do you think I

ended up winning over your mother?"

"Ew, Dad! Gross!" Ray said. "Do the Roswellians even *have* noses?"

"They must. Otherwise, how would they sneeze?"

"Hmm . . . Interesting point, Dad. Well, until we see one of the aliens sneezing, we need to get back to my friends. Any clue how we could find them?"

"Oh, don't you worry about that, Ray," Mr. Mond said. "Your dear old dad still has a few more tricks up his sleeve . . ."

He directed Ray over to yet another table covered with a large linen sheet. His dad unfurled the cover and revealed a wall of monitors much like the Central Brain that Director Harlow used back in the main hall.

"As the janitor, I have access to camera feeds and intercoms that reach every corner of this place," he explained. "You know . . . in case I need to find any puke to clean up."

Mr. Mond yanked open a drawer and pulled out a dusty old computer mouse. He plugged the mouse into the wall of monitors, sending a spark into the air.

"Whoa!" Ray's dad chuckled. "Guess it's been a while since I've used this thing!"

"You're saying we can use this to tap into the camera system?" Ray asked.

"From this janitor's closet, my boy," his dad explained, "we can see every single inch of Area 51."

CHAPTER TWELVE

Standing among the rubble of the damaged hallway, Elijah and Viv were at a loss for what to do next. With Ray and Charlotte missing, the two of them were completely alone together for the first time ever. Viv had just battled three fully grown hostile aliens and yet, somehow, felt more nervous now than she had all day.

"Guess it's just the two of us." Elijah chuckled.

"Um, I guess so . . . ," she replied, trying to hide the blush that was blooming in her cheeks. "I'm worried the aliens may have taken Charlotte as a hostage."

Elijah turned away from Viv to peer down the hallway toward where the Roswellians had glided off, his hand scratching at the back of his neck.

Is he nervous, too?

"Maybe if we go quick enough, we might be able to catch up with the Roswellians and take them by surprise," Elijah said.

Or just trying to ease the awkward silence?

Elijah turned back, and their eyes met. She stared into that beautiful, deep chestnut color that always clouded her dreams and—

"HEY! Are you guys gonna kiss, or what?" A voice echoed through the hall.

Viv and Elijah instinctually jumped into standing back-to-back with their weapons aimed in either direction.

But then recognition kicked in, and they both realized who the Australian-twanged voice belonged to.

"Up here!" Charlotte called out.

Viv and Elijah craned their heads back, following the sound of her voice toward the roof.

Charlotte's feet were planted firmly on the ceiling. Her long blond hair fell in a cascade like pale, yellow icicles as she smiled at them from above.

"Charlotte?!" they both shouted.

"The one and only!"

"Are you kidding me? How did you get on the ceiling?"

"With so many of me running around during the fight, it started getting a little confusing," Charlotte shouted down. "Even I wasn't sure which one of me was real! So I chewed a piece of my antigravity gum, and—"

"You've had antigravity gum this whole time?" Elijah erupted.

"I guess so!" Charlotte admitted. "I picked it up back in the

Gadgets Room, thinking it was just normal gum. But then I read the label. Plus, it's grape flavored!"

Charlotte spat out the gum, returning to the world's normal gravity orientation. She landed perfectly on her feet, like the world's most loudmouthed Olympic gymnast.

"Whoa! How does that stuff work?" Elijah asked.

"It's actually rather simple, my dear friend," Charlotte said smugly. She fished in her pocket and pulled out a small purple pack of gum.

"Chewing a piece flips your gravity upside down. Spitting it out flips you right side up. Simple!"

"Yeah, but how does it actually *work*?"

"Oh geez. I don't know!" Charlotte replied. "It sort of feels like what happens when you put the same poles of two magnets near each other. Ya know how they push against each other? I guess the gum flips your magnetic pole or something, so you repel Earth's gravity. Here, try a piece! And if you'd like more, it's just three easy payments of $19.99."

Elijah's eyes opened wide as he grabbed a stick. He unrolled the foil wrapping and popped the grape gum into his mouth. Instantly, his feet flipped out from under him. He flailed all the way up until he gained his balance on the ceiling.

"This is incredible!" Elijah said. "Not quite as cool as flying, but it's pretty dang close!"

"You want to try it, Viv?" Charlotte held out the pack.

Following Elijah's lead, Viv grabbed a piece and started

chewing. A floating feeling bubbled up through her body as the gum lifted her legs from beneath her, drifting her up toward the concrete. The metal foot coverings of her suit hit the ceiling with a clang.

"Whoa. This is awesome!" Viv shouted.

Charlotte popped in a new piece of gum and joined them on the ceiling. She flung her arms out, as if welcoming them to her domain.

"Right?" Charlotte smacked the gum in her mouth. "I had a bird's-eye view of the entire battle. Speaking of which . . ."

Charlotte turned to Viv with furrowed brows. "It looked like your arm cannon was completely broken by the end, Viv."

"Yeah, it was," she replied.

"So how did you fire off that last shot at Megdar? The really powerful green one that scared him away?"

Viv tried to think back to the terrible moment.

"I don't know. It all happened so fast." Viv shook her head. "I remember falling, and I remember Megdar grabbing Elijah. But then I closed my eyes . . ."

It hurt Viv to remember Elijah twisting in pain under the evil alien's grasp and the surge of anger that had taken hold of her. She felt a piercing headache coming on.

"Well, whatever you did, it was incredible!" Charlotte said, oblivious to Viv's reaction. "And how'd you make that energy blast green? The rest were purp—"

"I told you, I don't know!" Viv snapped, her head aching. It was bad enough that she'd accidentally hurt Elijah. Getting interrogated by Charlotte was the last thing she needed right now.

"Okay, geez, sorry." Charlotte put her hands up defensively.

"No matter what, we're gonna need that arm cannon working if we want a chance at beating Megdar," Elijah said, trying to calm the situation. "Is there anything you can do to fix it, Charlotte?"

"Of course," Charlotte said, crossing her arms across her chest. "If Viv promises not to bite me."

Viv's face softened. "I'm sorry, Char. I didn't mean to snap at you. And come on, I bit you *one time* in kindergarten. When are you gonna let that go?" She smiled and offered her arm cannon for inspection.

Charlotte laughed. "Only when you admit that you were peeking in that game of heads up, seven up!"

After turning it over a couple times and examining the damage, Charlotte cinched a few of the steel parts into place. Within seconds, the cannon revved back to life.

"There ya go, all better!"

"Wow!" Elijah exclaimed. "How'd you do that so fast?"

"I've been tinkering with homemade guitars for years, and considering a cannon doesn't even need to be tuned, it wasn't too tough to figure out."

"Think there's anything you can do about this dented wing, then?" he asked politely.

Charlotte reached out and wrapped her hands around the

crushed edge. She applied force onto two pressure points and popped the dent out with one loud snap. The wing looked good as new.

"Great work, Charlotte!"

"Thanks!" she replied. "I also do AC and refrigerator repair." She dusted off her hands and turned toward Viv and Elijah. "We should get going."

"But what about Ray? We've gotta find him!" Viv said.

"If he fell down that drain, he's probably halfway to Cleveland by now," Charlotte replied.

"Hmmm." Elijah pondered. "So, that means Ray is in Nebraska?"

Viv smiled. "No matter where he is, we've got to find him."

There's no way we're leaving any one of us behind.

A mechanical clack broke the silence. Charlotte and Elijah hit the deck—or in this case, the ceiling—flattening their bodies to blend in with the beams that supported the floor above. Viv aimed her cannon and swept it across their surroundings. Out of the corner of her eye, she caught a tiny hint of movement.

A security camera rotated slowly toward her. The eerie red light above the lens blinked on and off as it zeroed in on them.

"Don't . . . move . . . ," Viv instructed through clenched teeth.

Someone was watching them.

CHAPTER THIRTEEN

"There!" Ray shouted. "That's them!"

After combing through dozens of security cameras in and around the Gadgets Room—and after Ray had popped in an extra pair of contacts his dad had on hand in the closet—the duo finally found Viv, Charlotte, and Elijah.

Mr. Mond leaned in over the desk. He jostled the joystick to the left, adjusting the camera and zooming in on the three kids.

Ray tilted his head in confusion. Something about the camera feed on the monitors seemed off.

"What the . . ."

Ray bent over at his waist and peered from between his knees at the monitor. "Are they . . . upside down?" he wondered aloud.

"Must be something wrong with this hunk of junk," his dad huffed. Mr. Mond smacked his palm against the side of the monitor with frustration. The screen flashed to black-and-white static for a brief second before refocusing.

On-screen, Charlotte and Elijah lay flat on their backs on the ceiling. Viv stood on her feet, seemingly hanging upside down. Slowly, she raised her arm, pointing her cannon directly at the lens Mr. Mond was controlling.

Oh crud.

"No!" Ray exclaimed. "She's gonna destroy the camera!" He smacked at his father's arm. "Can you turn on the intercom so we can talk to them?"

"Uh, let me see . . ."

Ray watched as his father fidgeted with a few unmarked buttons on the desk. His eyes jolted back to the screen. Even in the fuzzy image, Ray could see the blast of energy forming within Viv's arm cannon. They were running out of time.

"Let me try!" Ray elbowed his father out of the way. He'd always had a knack for computers.

Ray's eyes flitted across the array of buttons. He could feel a drop of sweat pooling on his forehead. He took a deep breath and reached out, hoping his technological instincts would take care of the rest.

He picked a random switch and flipped it.

By some miracle, a dusty old microphone extended from the control panel. Ray heard the crackle of the audio kick in.

"Viv! Wait, don't shoot!" Ray called into the receiver.

On-screen, Viv's face twisted in recognition. She lowered her arm cannon and squinted at the camera. Her voice piped in through the garbled speaker in the janitor's closet.

"Ray?" Viv asked. "Is that you?!"

"Well, it ain't the Easter Bunny!"

On-screen, Charlotte's body jolted up from the ceiling.

"We thought you were in Nebraska!" Charlotte said.

"Where are you?" Elijah added.

"I'm with my dad!" Ray yelled into the microphone. "We're in the janitor's closet."

The three kids on-screen shared a surprised glance.

"Mr. Mond?" Viv said.

"I'm here, kids!" Mr. Mond chimed in.

"How did you get out of the main hall?" Elijah asked.

"Well, actually, I—"

"Hey, guys?" Ray cut in, not wanting his friends to know the truth about his dad fleeing from the danger. "Did the Earth flip upside down out there?"

"Kinda. We'll explain everything later," Viv said.

"Oh, that's all right, kids," Mr. Mond said. "I've worked at Area 51 for a long time. I've seen my fair share of weird stuff."

A duplicate of Charlotte popped into the frame, waving happily at the camera.

"Okay, that's the weirdest," Mr. Mond admitted.

"Mr. Mond?" Viv said. "Can you use the camera system to see where they're holding our parents?"

"I don't know, kids," Mr. Mond said. "I don't think we should be facing those aliens. What kind of adult would I be if I put you in harm's way like that?"

"We might not even need to fight them," Ray said. "Guys, I found Meekee!"

At the sound of his name, Meekee popped up out of Ray's pocket with delight.

"Meekee!" the little alien trilled into the microphone.

"Great job, Ray," Viv said with a smile.

"We can still give the Roswellians what they want. No one else needs to get hurt," Ray declared. "Dad, we just need you to help us find them."

"It's our only option," the two Charlottes said simultaneously.

Mr. Mond stared at the screen, examining each face of the three headstrong kids staring back at him. The determination in their eyes was clear. There was nothing that could stop them.

He heaved a deep, heavy sigh.

"If the aliens are meeting at their ship like Ray overheard, there's only one place they could be," he said, leaning in closer to the microphone. "The terrarium. It's the only part of Area 51 that's aboveground. The middle of it has a porthole with clear access to the sky for a launch."

"Where is that?" Viv asked.

"The big dome at the center of the complex," Mr. Mond explained. "You probably saw it on your way in. It's impossible to miss."

"It's a terrarium?" Charlotte asked. "What happens there?"

"It's split into a hundred different sectors, all with different creatures and terrains used for experimental testing."

"Sounds dangerous," Elijah said, revving his suit's engine.

"Oh, it is," Mr. Mond assured them. "And really hard to clean."

"How can they get there? Do you have a map of the compound somewhere in here?" Ray asked.

Mr. Mond smiled and tapped his index finger against his temple. "It's all up here, son." Mr. Mond beamed. "Your dad knows this place like the back of his fart gun."

On-screen, Elijah turned to Viv with a puzzled look.

"Wait, did he say fart gu—"

"If you kids are outside the Gadgets Room, you'll need to take the VERT Train and then cut through the terrarium."

"Take the *train*?" Viv asked. "There's a whole train system that runs through Area 51?"

"Anything beats crawling through the air vents behind Ray for an hour," Charlotte replied. "What are we waiting for? Let's go!"

Mr. Mond pushed aside the stacks of paper on his desk. He examined the map of the compound that was printed on the table, tracing his finger along the route from the Gadgets Room to the center of the terrarium.

"Oh no." Mr. Mond's voice dropped an octave.

"What is it, Dad?"

"The fastest way to get to the center of the terrarium is to cut straight through Sector 77 . . ." Mr. Mond hesitated.

"What's in Sector 77?" Viv asked.

The hairs on the back of Mr. Mond's neck stood straight up.

"Um . . . it's the *prehistoric* sector . . ."

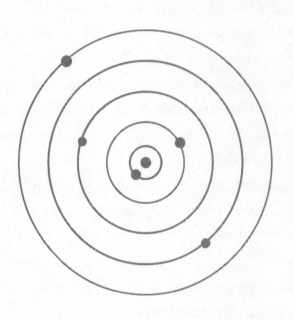

CHAPTER
FOURTEEN

"Prehistoric?" Charlotte asked, still smacking the antigravity gum after Mr. Mond had relayed the directions. "So what, we'll have to make friends with some cavemen or something? Shouldn't be too hard. I'm already friends with half of my dad's rugby team!"

There was no time to waste. Viv, Elijah, and Charlotte dashed along the ceiling past the Gadgets Room and down the hallway where Megdar and his cronies had escaped.

"You heard Mr. Mond," Viv said in a hushed tone. "He said he wasn't sure exactly what experiments were in Sector 77, but we should be prepared for anything."

The trio followed Mr. Mond's instructions, taking two lefts, then a right, followed by two more lefts. They tiptoed along the ceiling in a crouched stance, being sure to stay quiet and vigilant. They passed by door after door of unmarked rooms. Viv could only imagine what kind of top secret experiments lurked behind each one.

She could feel the blood rushing to her head. Viv realized this was the longest time she'd ever spent upside down. Maybe the longest time anyone had spent upside down.

One more turn, and we should be there.

Mr. Mond had instructed them to look for a train station. The VERT, he called it.

"I can't believe they can fit a whole subway inside this place!" Viv whispered.

"You just battled a bunch of huge aliens from another planet, and you're impressed by a choo choo?" Charlotte laughed.

As they curved around the last turn of ceiling, Viv peered around the corner. She yanked her head back.

A pair of Roswellian scouts hovered below, only a few yards beneath them.

All three kids froze.

Viv lifted her index finger to her lips. Elijah and Charlotte nodded. She stretched her neck, peeking out just enough to see a sliver of the next corridor.

She had never seen the Roswellians from this vantage point before. From the ground, the aliens were a slithering mass of frightening green tentacles covered in a thousand blinking eyes. But from above, Viv made a key observation about her enemy.

They can't see us up here.

Viv lowered her voice to an almost imperceptible whisper

and leaned in close to Elijah and Charlotte.

"Their eyes only point downward," she reported. "If we're quiet enough, we can sneak right above them."

"Good plan. You go first," Charlotte whispered back.

Viv looked back at the two behemoths below. She took a deep breath.

"Follow me," she instructed, taking the first few steps out around the corner.

The Roswellians buzzed beneath her, floating back and forth between each of the corridor's entry points, scanning each hallway like two hideous bloodhounds.

They're searching for us.

The metal of Viv's combat suit clanged against the ceiling ever so slightly. She stopped dead in her tracks.

The Roswellians still rotated aimlessly below.

She let out a silent sigh of relief.

She shuffled her feet instead, careful not to make a single peep. After a few more steps, she made it safely around the corner and finally let out the breath she'd been holding.

She peered back to check on Elijah's progress. His flight suit had soft mesh along the soles, so he was able to scurry along the ceiling silently. Viv reached out her hand, helping him around the corner and into safety.

Come on, Charlotte.

Charlotte scampered along the ceiling with ease. She had seemingly catlike reflexes and looked much more comfortable being upside down than Viv did.

She was a few steps away. Viv and Elijah watched, holding their breath. They were so close to reaching the train.

Just as Charlotte was passing above the second of the massive aliens, Viv's heart almost stopped.

Oh no! Her hair!

Charlotte's long blond hair was about to graze the top of the taller Roswellian. Viv tried to think of some way to divert the alien's attention. But Charlotte was already way ahead of her.

"Hey! Over here!" a voice called out from the opposite entrance of the corridor.

The Roswellians spun around in a whirl. They zeroed in on the Charlotte clone that was waving at them from across the room.

Charlotte grabbed her locks by the fistful and yanked them up at the last second, an inch from giving herself away.

The Roswellians rushed toward the duplicate, who took off running down the hallway.

"That should keep them busy for a while." Charlotte smiled as she rounded the corner.

With the Roswellians safely distracted far away down the corridor, Viv and Elijah spat out their gum and landed on the ground with a thud. Charlotte angled her neck and spat her gum into a recycling bin. It was actually quite an impressive shot.

"Hey, gum doesn't go in the recycling bin," Viv pointed out.

"You're just jealous that I'm the LeBron James of spitting gum," Charlotte said.

The wad of gum stuck against the side of the container, sending the recycling bin flying upside down. It clanged against the ceiling as old coffee cups and crumpled papers poured out, raining down onto the floor.

"Huh! I guess the gum works on objects, too!" Charlotte laughed.

Viv stepped over a few candy wrappers and an empty box of mints before turning the last corner.

Yes! We made it.

A majestic glowing sign above the hallway in front of them spelled out their destination: "The VERT Train."

The kids scurried through and checked over their shoulders, making sure no one was following them. Huge sliding glass doors flanked the platform's entrance.

Elijah grabbed one, Viv grabbed the other, and they pushed them together until the latches gently clicked into place. They each took a deep breath, feeling safe for the first time in a while.

The VERT Train platform was sleek and futuristic. Glowing arrows on the floor pulsed with neon blue light, each of them pointing toward a cabin door. The train itself looked like a polished steel bullet, with every edge you'd normally see on a traditional train smoothed down to a glossy curve. It looked wicked fast.

Viv walked up to the mechanical wonder.

Wow. Once we get her back, I really gotta ask Mom for a full tour of this place.

"How do we get the doors to open?" Elijah wondered.

Viv examined the side of the train. Foreign symbols inscribed into the steel side glowed blue in rhythm with the idle hum of the engine. Her eyes landed on a small screen beside the cabin door.

A scanner.

Viv placed her palm against the cold glass. A turquoise light passed from the heel of her palm up to her fingertips.

An automated woman's voice played through the scanner. Her tone was robotic yet somehow calming.

"DNA cannot be traced. Please place an acceptable DNA sample onto scanner."

"DNA?" Viv wondered aloud.

Viv went over her options in her head. She smiled to herself, laughing at the idea of what she was about to do.

"How about this?" Viv answered the automated woman.

Viv hocked the biggest loogie in the universe onto the scanner.

"Saliva sample accepted. DNA confirmed. Welcome, Director Cassandra Harlow."

It thinks I'm my mom!

One of the four glass train doors slid open.

Elijah flashed Viv a grin. He quickly followed her lead, slapping his tongue right onto the detector by the next train door.

"DNA confirmed. Welcome, Lieutenant Nicolás Padilla."

"Is this considered identity theft?" Elijah laughed.

"I think it's okay if we're saving their lives," Charlotte said. She smirked, and then sneezed so hard onto the third scanner, she nearly cracked it.

"Welcome, Dr. Sabrina Frank," the automated voice announced.

"Ha!" Charlotte exclaimed. "I must sneeze just like my mom!"

The trio exchanged quick nods and then stepped into the train car.

The interior of the VERT Train looked like a luxury yacht. Rows of velvet cushioned benches and plasma screens lined the titanium walls, and they could feel the power of the train thrumming beneath their feet.

"Now, THIS is how to get around the office!" Charlotte whooped. "I can't believe our parents get to ride this thing every day!"

She slid into the very last row, already making herself at home. "Cool kids sit in the back!"

"The coolest kids figure out how to get this train moving," Viv said.

Viv walked down the aisle of the train car toward the front compartment. The glass windshield of the locomotive looked out onto complete darkness.

"Let's get this show on the road!" Charlotte's voice echoed up to the front. She had already kicked her feet up and was fiddling with the seltzer water dispenser embedded in the train's wall.

Viv examined the massive control panel in front of her. Lights and buttons vibrated and flashed in complicated sequences that she couldn't decipher.

"What's the holdup?" Charlotte pestered.

"I don't know, Char," Viv said sarcastically. "Do you have experience driving what's probably a hypersonic train from the future?"

"A train is a train, right?"

Viv stuck her tongue out in response.

"Oh, don't be such a wet kangaroo!"

"I'll come take a look," Elijah offered, before joining Viv in the engineer's compartment. He surveyed the console for a moment and then let out a short gasp.

"Wait a second . . ." Elijah's voice lifted. "These controls are super similar to some of the flight simulator video games my dad has at home. He lets me play with them sometimes."

"Great! Do you think you can start it up?" Viv asked, praying the answer was yes.

"Let's give her a try," Elijah said confidently.

Elijah pressed a few buttons, pulled down on a large steel lever, and twisted the key in the ignition.

The train roared to life beneath their feet. Viv couldn't contain the smile spreading across her cheeks. They were one step closer to getting their parents back.

"VERT Train engine: activated." A robotic voice chimed up over the speaker.

Elijah imitated the train system's automated voice. "Where would you like to go, Director Harlow?" he asked with a smirk.

"Terrarium Sector 77, please, Lieutenant Padilla," Viv said, playing along.

Elijah typed the coordinates into the keyboard, and the same automated voice rang out over the train's speaker system. "Destination located. Next stop: Terrarium Sector 77."

"FINALLY!" Charlotte griped from the backseat, sipping a tall glass of seltzer. She sprawled across the bench like she owned the place. "I'll take the filet, medium well, please."

Elijah returned to the front seat. Viv scooted in next to him, remembering all the times in elementary school she was too nervous to sit by him on the bus.

Elijah leaned back and hollered toward Charlotte, "You sure you're not lonely back there?"

"I'm doing lovely!" Charlotte said, flipping through the channels on the plasma screen. "And I'll have the crème brûlée for dessert, please."

The automated voice chirped up.

"Please put on your seat belts. Place all service items away and prepare for departure."

The seat belts dropped out of the ceiling. They were heavy-duty straps of dark gray nylon and a thick steel buckle crisscrossed into a bulky harness, clearly designed for the body of an adult. After some strap tightening and maneuvering, Elijah and Viv clicked theirs into place.

Viv whirled her head around. Charlotte was still lounging across her bench.

"Charlotte, put your seat belt on," Viv reminded her.

"Seat belt? This thing is like a straitjacket!" Charlotte argued, pulling at the hanging belts. "Plus, it's just a train. I'll be fi—"

The robotic woman's voice cut her off.

"Departing from the station in T minus ten. Nine—"

Their seats began to rumble.

"Eight."

"Charlotte, I really think you should put the seat belt on," Viv said.

"Seven."

"But it looks uncomfortable!" Charlotte whined.

"Six."

"Charlotte!"

"Five."

"Ugh, fine." Charlotte snapped the buckle into place across her chest.

"Four."

"I wonder why they call it the VERT Train . . . ," Charlotte mused aloud.

"Three."

The pungent smell of jet fuel stung their noses.

"Elijah, did you turn on your flight suit?" Viv asked.

"Two."

"No?"

"One."

Metal clanging rang out through the cabin. The rumbling beneath their seats turned into an intense shaking.

"Liftoff."

"Liftoff?" all three of them shouted.

The train platform tilted backward ninety degrees, lifting the entire train tracks vertically into the air. Their backs pressed into the seats and their feet dangled helplessly.

Viv clutched her stomach, worried she might lose what little breakfast she'd eaten that morning.

The train exploded from the station like a rocket. The intense velocity made it feel like the world's most extreme roller coaster. Charlotte's seltzer water spewed through the cabin in suspended bubbles.

Viv strained her neck to the right and saw Elijah's cheeks flapping from the g-force.

"AHHHHHH!" Viv felt like a piece of Jell-O on a slingshot. Even though the entire ride lasted only a few seconds, it seemed like they were in motion for ages, practically shooting off into space.

Finally, the train jerked to a halt. The comforting tone of the automated voice now felt bizarrely out of place.

"Now arriving at Terrarium Sector 77."

Viv felt the back of her head slam into the cushioned headrest. Mechanical hissing and decompression sounds rang out through the cabin as the train returned to a horizontal position.

For a long moment, Viv could only hear the slight ringing in her ears from the takeoff. Then—

"WOOOOO!" Elijah lifted his arms into the air. "That was incredible!"

Just like his dad, he'd always been an adrenaline junkie. Viv tried to catch her breath in the seat next to him.

"Are you guys okay?" Elijah asked, suddenly realizing he might've been the only one enjoying the ride.

"I feel like we just slingshot around the sun and went back in time," Viv squeaked. She swiveled her head around toward the rear of the cabin.

Charlotte was drenched in seltzer. Her usually straight, silky hair sat in a knotted dripping mess atop her head. The smile she had just moments ago had faded into a rigid frown.

Viv laughed at the sight. "Who's the wet kangaroo now?"

She fumbled with the heavy straps of the harness that kept her pinned to the seat. Elijah, already free from his own seat belt, reached over and helped unbuckle Viv. Charlotte untangled herself from the mess of straps that she'd clicked into place at the last second. Though she would never admit it, Viv's advice probably saved her life.

"Anyone else feel like their brain got squished into their feet?" Charlotte asked woozily. "Let's never do that again. And I'm not complaining, but I never got my crème brûlée."

Before anyone could even fix their hair, the glass doors of the train car unlatched with a loud clack.

The three kids whipped their heads around. The doors slowly slid open, revealing a sprawling prehistoric jungle that looked like it was sixty-five million years old.

"Uh-oh . . . ," Charlotte said. "Definitely no cavemen in here . . ."

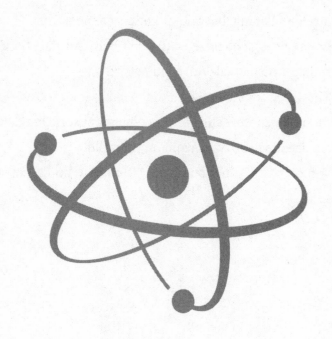

CHAPTER
FIFTEEN

A wave of heat and humidity engulfed Viv as she took her first step out of the VERT Train and onto the jungle floor. She could feel the sweat forming on her forehead already.

She craned her head back. Enormous trees towered above, their canopies covering where the sky should be. Vines swayed in complicated loops around each massive wooden trunk. Birds cawed from the treetops and the low hum of insects made Viv's skin crawl. The air reeked of wet soil with the tiniest hint of sweetness.

She marveled at the technological wonder of it all. The dome of the terrarium sat high above them. But Viv felt like she was outside on a different planet, in a completely different era.

Wow. And to think just a few hours ago, I thought space coconuts would be the coolest thing I'd see all day.

Viv held her arm cannon at the ready. Elijah followed close behind, the engine of his flight suit rumbling on his lower back.

CLANG!

Viv whipped around. The doors of the VERT Train slammed shut. The bright lights shining from the train's interior moments ago had blended into the bark of a tall tree, leaving them stranded in the darkness of the dim jungle floor. Like everything else in Area 51, the train was able to cloak itself in high-tech camouflage.

There's no turning back now.

Viv swiveled around to find Charlotte had already dashed ahead.

"Guys!" Charlotte's voice echoed through the trees. "Check this out!"

Charlotte stood below the biggest banana Viv had ever seen. It was twice the size of her body, and she was the tallest one of their group.

Elijah walked up to investigate the monster fruit. "I don't wanna see the monkey who eats that!"

"Imagine slipping on this peel!" Charlotte added. "You'd be falling forever!"

"I don't think that's how it works." Viv laughed.

"If this is what a banana looks like, I don't wanna see a watermelon."

"We better keep moving," Elijah cautioned, shifting his eyes across the treetops, searching for any signs of danger.

The trio trekked through the thick brush. They tiptoed on top of the leafy floor below them, careful not to crunch any twigs or trip over rocks. A mistake now could give them away to the Roswellians . . . or to whatever else was lurking in this jungle.

Just then, Charlotte's ears perked up. "Listen." She hushed the others.

The sound of a nearby waterfall thundered in Viv's eardrums.

"It sounds close. We should stop for a drink," Charlotte said. "I'm dying of thirst."

"Didn't you just have a drink on the train?" Viv asked.

"Yeah, and I'm wearing it! Remember?"

Viv smacked the dry roof of her mouth with her tongue. She tried to think back to when she last had a sip of water. Pure adrenaline had been pushing her through the entire day, and it seemed like the exhaustion in her body had finally caught up to her.

"Okay," Viv said. "We can stop for a quick second, but then we need to keep moving."

The trio followed the sound of the water through another mile of jungle. Viv led the way as they passed below huge ginkgo trees, maneuvered around thick ferns, and splashed through shallow puddles. Charlotte marched twenty yards behind, swatting at bugs like a madwoman. Elijah trotted a few steps to catch up with Viv.

"Hey." His voice grew louder as he settled in stride next to Viv. "I guess I owe you an official thank-you."

"For what?" Viv asked, still scanning the trees to avoid

making eye contact with Elijah.

"For saving my life back in the hallway," Elijah said. "That alien would've squeezed me into chicken noodle soup if it wasn't for you."

Viv smiled. "It could've been worse," she said. "He could've squeezed you into clam chowder, and nobody likes that stuff."

Elijah laughed a little too loud but caught himself before the noise could echo that much.

"Plus, it's no big deal," Viv continued. "I know you would have done the same for me."

Elijah smiled and nodded, his white teeth glowing in the slivers of light that shone down through the breaks in the treetops. They walked in silence for a moment.

"You know, I can't stop thinking about my dad," he said, his voice turning serious.

"I know what you mean," Viv agreed. "I'm worried about my mom, too."

"I wouldn't be," Elijah said. "Your mom is unstoppable. She's tougher than the aliens!"

Viv chuckled. Her mom had a commanding presence even when she wasn't being the director of the largest secret government base in the world.

Elijah sighed. "From the time I was a baby, it was just me and my dad. He was at every baseball game, every parent-teacher night, whenever I needed him. And now he needs me."

Viv's thoughts drifted to her own father, the man she'd

never met. Her mom almost never talked about him, and she didn't keep any photos of him in the house, either. But that didn't stop Viv from imagining a perfect version of him.

In her mind, Viv felt like she knew everything about him. From his weekends spent watching sports to his out-of-tune but joyous singing. Even his love of barbecue food. All of it made Viv feel like he was real. Like he was there.

But in reality, the only thing Viv knew for certain was that he and her mom met as employees at the compound. It was the one piece of information about her dad that she'd managed to coax out of her mother, besides the fact that he wasn't coming back.

It made being at Area 51 all the weirder to Viv, knowing that he used to walk these halls. And now she faced the horrible possibility that this place would claim the only parent she had left.

The two kids climbed over an enormous fallen tree covered in thick, fuzzy moss, the silence still lingering between them.

Viv heard Elijah sniffle, and she turned to see him wipe the beginnings of a tear from his eye. Viv had never seen this side of him before. He was usually so confident and self-assured.

"We're gonna find him, Elijah," Viv said. "I know it. Don't worry."

"Thanks, Viv," Elijah whispered.

His footsteps halted for a moment. Something on the

jungle floor had caught his eye. Viv stopped and leaned in to see what he was doing.

Elijah knelt down by a thorn-covered bush. Out of the sharp stems, shimmering silver and yellow flowers bloomed. Elijah wrapped his palms around the delicate petals and looked up at Viv.

No way. Is he . . . ?

Viv had never been given a flower from a boy. Now that she thought about it, she'd never gotten anything from a boy.

Elijah carefully plucked the shimmering blossom from the vine and examined it for a moment.

Viv's breath caught in her chest.

Then Elijah stuffed the flower into his mouth.

He ate it? You've got to be kidding me!

"My dad used to be deployed in the jungle when he was in the Air Force. He taught me which plants are good and which are bad," mumbled Elijah. "These ones are edible."

"What?" Viv asked. It was hard to understand him with his mouth full. Elijah choked down the last petal with one final gulp. From the twisted expression on his face, Viv could tell the taste wasn't worth all the chewing.

"You can eat the flowers!" Elijah clarified.

Viv sheepishly laughed and turned to keep walking ahead, but Charlotte's voice stopped her.

"Yes, finally!" Charlotte called out from a few yards back.

Elijah and Viv turned around.

Charlotte pressed her hands between two thick patches of leaves and parted the branches. Beyond her extended arms, a huge clearing opened up. The sound was unmistakable.

The waterfall.

A torrent of water roared off an enormous cliff to the right. Giant yellow lotus flowers floated along the river that spilled from beneath the rushing downpour. The edges of the water were clouded beneath mangrove overgrowths.

The kids ducked in below the vines. Viv instantly felt the streams of late-afternoon sunlight reflecting off the water warm her skin. They must have been in the jungle for a while now.

Charlotte sped ahead, kneeling down on the riverbank. She yanked her left hand out of her gauntlet, plunged it into the sparkling water, and lapped up the water from her palm like a dehydrated golden retriever.

Viv and Elijah started to follow her but then immediately froze.

"Guys! You have to try this!" Charlotte yelled between huge gulps. "It tastes just like water!"

"Charlotte . . . ," Elijah whispered.

"Come have a sip!" She beckoned.

"Stay very still," he breathed.

"What?" Charlotte said impatiently, before twisting to look up to her left.

Turned out she'd chosen the wrong side of the river.

A massive scaly leg led to a massive scaly body, which led up to a massive scaly face, lapping up water right next to Charlotte.

Viv stared at the creature.

Is that a . . . It can't be a . . .

"Yep," Viv said in pure amazement. "That's a *Stegosaurus*."

Among the tree leaves, the dinosaur's rough green skin blended in perfectly. Huge bony plates jutted straight out of its spine. Viv's eyes followed the plates down to its tail swaying in the air behind, embedded with razor-sharp spikes.

Charlotte's jaw hung wide open, spilling out the water she'd collected.

"Charlotte," Viv cautioned. "Don't panic. Just don't move."

Viv didn't need to worry about that, as Charlotte was clearly frozen in fear.

"It's a leaf eater," Viv explained under her breath. "And last I checked, you're not a leaf. It won't hurt us, unless someone—"

Charlotte let out an ear-piercing scream.

"—disturbs it."

The *Stegosaurus* reared up onto its hind legs in surprise, the bony plates along its spine causing numerous mangroves to topple. In the chaos, Charlotte scrambled back to the clearing, where Viv and Elijah ducked behind a tree stump.

The dinosaur let out a low, fearful bellow before slamming its front legs back down into the muddy soil of the riverbank.

Water and sludge splattered in the kids' direction. The giant beast thrashed its spiky tail a few times, turned its back, and galloped through the brush and out of sight.

Charlotte clung to Viv's armor like a baby. Even through the metal, Viv could feel Charlotte's heart pounding in her chest.

As the sound of the dinosaur's heavy footsteps faded off into the distance, the clearing slowly returned to silence aside from the flowing waterfall.

Elijah and Viv met each other's gaze for a moment. Then they burst into laughter.

"Oh, knock it off, you blokes!"

"You didn't have to scare it off like that!" Viv insisted. "That poor guy is a vegetarian!"

"Just because it eats leaves doesn't mean it can't kill you!" Charlotte protested. "Ever heard of getting stomped on? I once heard about a guy who got squished by an elephant and *then* the elephant ate him!"

Elijah and Viv just laughed harder.

"You're missing the point," Charlotte shouted. "There are DINOSAURS in this jungle! It would've been nice if Mr. Mond had told us THAT!"

That quickly made Viv stop laughing.

She's right. If a Stegosaurus is here, that means there could be less friendly dinosaurs, too . . .

The three of them trekked on for another twenty minutes,

⁂ 133 ⁂

now even more cautiously. This time, Charlotte wasn't taking any chances. She slipped on her gauntlets and materialized ten Farlottes out of thin air. With the clones acting as a human shield, the eleven Charlottes hollered in unison, scaring away any of the smaller and more docile creatures hiding in the fields ahead.

A strange group of tiny lizards scurried across the jungle floor. Their colorful scales transitioned into what looked like long, peacock-like feathers along their backs.

"What the heck are those things?" Elijah asked.

"*Longisquama*," Viv said matter-of-factly.

Elijah and Charlotte looked at her like she was speaking a foreign language.

"What?" Viv said. "Didn't you guys pay attention in Mr. Cole's biology class?"

"Musta missed the class about *Love Your Mama*," Charlotte said.

"*Long-is-quama!*" Viv repeated. "Consider ourselves lucky that these are the only things we've run into so far."

"Yeah, thanks to all dozen of me!" Charlotte pointed out. "Elijah, can you fly up top and see how close we are to the center?"

Elijah lifted his wrist. The arrow indicating the fuel bar on his control display hovered just above the end marked "Empty."

"I'm almost out of juice," Elijah said. "If I go up there and hover for too long, I might not have enough to use later."

Viv looked down to the dented arm cannon on her own wrist. She wondered if it had enough power left to make it through the rest of their journey.

An unknown sound suddenly reverberated through the trees.

"What is that?" Charlotte panicked. "Another *Stegosaurus*? I'll chop him up and throw him on the barbie!"

She opened her mouth to shout, but Viv clapped a hand over her lips before any more sound could escape.

This noise wasn't coming from a dinosaur. It sounded more mechanical in nature.

"Elijah?" Viv suggested. "I think it might be worth the fuel to check it out."

Elijah considered it for a moment before glancing up at an ancient pine tree towering above to their left.

"Okay, you're right," Elijah agreed. "I'll take a quick flight to perch up on the top of that tree and see what I can find out."

With the push of a button, he extended the bright orange wings from his flight suit. He revved the engine and zoomed up, up, and away.

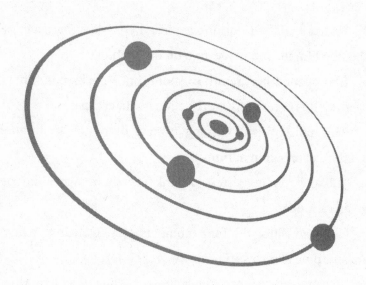

CHAPTER SIXTEEN

Within seconds, Elijah had flown up a hundred feet into the air. Charlotte and Viv shrunk to the size of ants on the ground below.

The tree was unimaginably tall. He might as well be climbing the Eiffel Tower. He held out his arms in front of his head, pushing needles and pine cones out of the way before they could whip him in the face.

Finally, a light broke through the treetops. He hovered above a sturdy-looking branch and gently set his feet down on the limb.

Elijah gasped. From this vantage point, he could see everything across the enormous terrarium.

Each sector was marked with a clear border. The one beside their slice of jungle was a sprawling sandy desert. Beyond that, a slice of ocean water broke in violent, tsunami-size waves. To their right, an icy tundra extended far off behind him. Every kind of environment on Earth was represented by a separate, breathtaking sector.

Above it all, the sky was covered by a huge, thick glass dome. His eyes traced the diameter of the terrarium's circle to its natural center. There it was: the porthole.

At the dome's tallest point, a small opening in the glass connected the hundreds of worlds in the terrarium with the world outside. By now, the Nevada sun had dipped below the horizon. A purplish twilight glow spilled in from the sky above.

Elijah barely had a chance to take in the scene before he registered something just below the picturesque sky and gasped.

Beneath the porthole's opening, what could only be described as a colossal spaceship hovered in the dusky light.

Even from a distance, Elijah could make out fast-moving blobs floating to and from the ship.

The Roswellians.

We found them.

CHAPTER SEVENTEEN

Viv watched as Elijah landed on the ground with a thud. He retracted his metal wings into the holster on his back.

"We're close, all of the Roswellians are just a little farther up," Elijah relayed while picking twigs and needles out of the mesh on his flight suit.

"You saw it? The spaceship?" Viv inquired.

Elijah nodded. "It's hovering below the porthole, right where Mr. Mond predicted. It's just up there, that way," he said, pointing through the trees.

"Then let's go! It's about time!" Charlotte motioned in the same direction.

"We should stay quiet," Elijah whispered.

"How many were there?" Viv asked. "Do you think we can take them?"

Elijah uncomfortably cleared his throat and kicked at some dirt on the ground.

"There were . . . a lot," he stammered.

"A lot?" Viv pressed. "How many is a lot? Fifty? Sixty?"

Elijah looked down at his feet.

"Elijah?"

"I'd say over a hundred aliens," he admitted.

The three friends just stared at each other for a long moment. The jungle seemed to grow silent around them.

Charlotte's voice broke the quiet. "Okay, good luck!" She turned around and started trotting back the way they came in.

"What?" Viv huffed. "You're leaving?"

"Um, duh! Of course I'm leaving!" Charlotte yelled over her shoulder. "We barely beat three of them. How are we supposed to take on a hundred?"

"You're the one who's been reckless this whole time," Viv argued. "And now you want to turn back? What happened to saving our parents? What happened to being brave?"

"This isn't bravery, Viv. It's stupidity!" Charlotte dug her feet into the dirt and turned to face her friend.

"What about your parents?" Elijah retorted.

"My dad apparently designs alien-fighting weapons for a living, and I'm guessing my mom works with stuff that's so scary, she's not even allowed to talk about it," Charlotte said. "If *they* can't take down an army of aliens, what makes you think we can?"

"But now? After all we've been through? I didn't think we'd make it out of that air vent!" Viv confessed. "But look how far we've come. I'm telling you, we've got luck on our side."

"Then good luck with your luck!" Charlotte flipped her hair and continued storming off.

"Charlotte, *where* are you going?"

"I'm going HOME!" Charlotte shouted at the top of her lungs.

"You won't have a home to go to!" Viv yelled, matching her volume.

"At least I'll be alive!" Charlotte shot back. "And honestly, having your parents get kidnapped by aliens is a pretty cool story. I'll tell everyone in class how you two—"

"Shh!" Viv hissed.

"Don't shush me," Charlotte snapped. "I'm serious, I'll—"

"Hold on! Be quiet!" Viv held up her finger. "Do you hear that?"

Everyone held their breath. A low growl echoed through the trees.

The ground beneath Viv's feet began to rumble. Small rock formations around them crumbled and fell to the ground.

Viv finally recognized the rhythmic thumping sound as it got closer and closer.

They're footsteps.

Something colossal was coming in their direction. And whatever it was, it was approaching fast.

Suddenly, an earsplitting roar sliced through the air. A flock of pterodactyls flew out of the treetops at the sound.

Viv covered her ears to block the noise. As the roar faded,

the jungle returned to an unsettling silence.

"What was *that*?" Elijah whispered.

"Like I said, good luck!" Charlotte waved and started toward the VERT Train.

"Charlotte! Wait!"

"A bunch of vegetarian dinosaurs don't scare me as much as those aliens do," Charlotte said. "I'll take my chances with them."

Just as Charlotte reached into the brush to go back the way they'd come, the leaves parted a few feet above her head.

A pair of tiny arms poked out through the branches.

"See?" Charlotte shouted back to Viv and Elijah. She stood on her tiptoes and baby-talked the hidden creature.

"That's a big noise coming from such a cute little—"

The treetops rustled far above Charlotte's head.

Two rows of daggerlike teeth slid out through the leaves. A leathery eye quickly followed. The huge circular pupil tightened its focus on the loud blond girl below.

This time, it wasn't a leaf eater.

It was a fully grown *Tyrannosaurus rex*.

The gargantuan beast loomed just a few feet above Charlotte. It let out a low growl and took a step forward, sending a tremor through the ground.

"Crikey . . ." Charlotte stumbled back. This time around, she didn't scream. She went into survival mode.

She clenched her fist within her gauntlet, causing clones to appear all around her. They pounced onto the massive lizard and started slamming punches into the creature's rough hide.

The *T. rex* let out another sinister roar. With one whip of its huge tail, it sent eight clones flying into the canopy.

Viv charged up a blast in her arm cannon. She reared back and aimed her palm toward the beast's head.

The *T. rex* whipped its tail again, this time in Viv and Elijah's direction. Elijah ducked and rolled out of the way just in time. But before she could get a precise shot, the tail slammed into Viv's suit. She rocketed through the air and crashed into a tree, directly onto her arm.

An uncontrolled purple blast flew out of Viv's palm. The energy ball erupted against the *T. rex*'s chest, pushing him back through the trees.

The beast let out a pained growl before stomping toward them again. The blast wasn't enough.

"Hit it harder!" Charlotte shouted.

The *T. rex* stepped closer, each footstep bouncing Viv into the air. Charlotte and Elijah rushed over to flank Viv.

"It's not working!" Viv slapped at the pieces of her arm cannon. It was shattered.

She tensed the muscles in her arm to pull the trigger, but instead felt an intense pain. She clutched her elbow.

The beast let out another thunderous roar—this time, so close that Viv could count the rows of teeth in the monster's mouth.

Specks of long, sticky saliva spewed out from the *T. rex*'s throat and landed on Charlotte with a splat.

"Elijah!" Viv shouted in between pained breaths. "Get us out of here!"

Elijah scooped up Charlotte and hooked Viv over his shoulder, careful not to squeeze too tightly on her injured arm. The engine on his flight suit rumbled to life. He kicked his feet off the ground and tried to propel them into the air. They hovered for a brief second before gravity pulled them back to the ground.

"No!" Elijah shouted. "The suit's running too low on fuel to carry all of us!"

The *T. rex* lowered its head, inches away from the base of the tree where the three kids were huddled. They held each other tight.

The beast's reptilian nostrils flared up and down, taking in a deep whiff of the three unfortunate kids destined to be its next meal.

This is it.

All of this, just to get eaten by a creature that went extinct millions of years ago. The irony almost made Viv want to laugh.

She looked over to Elijah and Charlotte. The fear in their eyes was paralyzing.

Viv felt a tear roll down her own cheek.

She closed her eyes and held her breath, ready for the end . . .

CHAPTER EIGHTEEN

"EAT FARTS, YOU STUPID LIZARD!"

Ray screamed at the top of his lungs as he and his father burst through the hidden drainpipe tucked beneath the deep foliage of the jungle floor. Meekee clung to the edge of Ray's shirt pocket, letting out a battle cry of his own.

"MEEKEE!"

Viv couldn't believe her eyes. Was she dreaming?

Did I already get eaten? Is heaven a place where Ray yells about farts?

The dinosaur's mouth roared open inches from her face. The skin connecting its jaws stretched to an extreme, ready to swallow its meal in a single gulp.

As his feet hit the soil, Ray pulled the trigger on the makeshift gun. Despite its junky appearance, the O.D.O.R. worked like a charm.

An overwhelming cloud of noxious green gas spilled from the rifle's barrel and engulfed the ancient reptile. The fart fumes flooded into the beast's slit nostrils. It wrenched its neck back and forth, trying desperately to shake off the mega stink.

Its massive pupils rolled back into its head. With one more deep inhale, the *T. rex* fainted. It hit the ground with an earth-trembling thwack, crashing into two trees on its way down. Its scaly body collapsed in a heap on the ground.

"Taken down by the power of farts!" Ray exclaimed. "That's what you get for trying to eat my friends!"

The three terrified kids huddled against the pine trunk took their first deep breath in minutes. Unfortunately, that breath of air still had a lingering whiff of yuck.

"Ray!" Elijah propped himself up onto one knee and pinched his nose. "How did you find us?"

Ray smiled ear to ear, resting the O.D.O.R. on his shoulder like a seasoned soldier. He would've looked like a superhero . . . if he hadn't been covered in mud and wearing nothing but racecar undies.

"We got here the janitor's way," Ray said, beaming. "Even the prehistoric jungle has sewage drains. And my dad knows them like the back of his hand. Right, Dad?"

Mr. Mond was still squeezing his way out of the drain. He finally squirmed free and took a step toward the kids.

"That's right!" he huffed, out of breath.

A fern wrapped around Mr. Mond's ankle. He tripped and landed face-first into the soil.

"Ouch." Charlotte covered her eyes. "That looks like it hurt."

Mr. Mond picked himself, dusted off the dirt, and carefully stepped around the *T. rex*'s limp body.

"Is it . . . dead?" Elijah asked.

The *T. rex* let out a snore-like huff. Everyone jumped.

Ray wasted no time and sprang into action. He reached into his shirt pocket and pulled out one of the sonic grenades Charlotte gave to him. He ripped the pin out with his teeth.

"Wait!" Charlotte yelled out.

But it was too late. Ray launched the grenade through the air with his full force.

He hit his target. The grenade flew right into the *T. rex*'s mouth, rattling off a few teeth in the bottom row before settling on its tongue.

For a second it was quiet.

Ray inspected the remaining grenade in his other hand.

"Do these things even wor—"

The grenade in the *T. rex*'s mouth exploded in a rainbow of colors. The sound was so loud and so fast that Viv's ears barely had time to register it.

A spinning hole of blazing black light emerged out of thin air from within the beast's jaws. Viv shielded her eyes with her uninjured arm.

A wormhole.

The dark, twisting corkscrew of antimatter grew bigger, sucking in loose leaves and small pebbles from the surrounding area.

The dinosaur's body contorted and shrunk. It spiraled into

the wormhole like water down a drain.

And just like that, the *T. rex* vanished, teleported through the rip in the space-time continuum that Ray had split open. The wormhole collapsed on itself with one final twinkle.

"Chew on THAT!" Ray shouted at the void, adrenaline coursing through his body.

"Ray, I think you might've gone a tad overboard," Viv replied.

Charlotte wandered over to the clear spot in the brush where the *T. rex* had lain just a moment ago. She grasped at the air.

"Ray . . ." Charlotte hesitated. "Do you know where those wormholes spit things out?"

"No?" Ray's pride transformed into uncertainty. "Where?"

"No, I'm asking." Charlotte whirled around. "I don't know, either."

"Eh." Ray brushed it off. "I'm sure with all of the different dimensions of space and time, we should be fine."

Mr. Mond leaned down to Elijah and Viv beside the tree trunk. He gently lifted Viv's arm into the air and examined it. She flinched at the sharp twinge of pain caused by the movement.

"It looks like you might have broken something in your arm, Viv," Mr. Mond concluded.

"I promise I'm okay," Viv said, her voice steely.

She pulled away from Mr. Mond and tried to prop herself up. More pain shot up her wrist, and she fell back down into the leaves.

"Viv . . . I'm sorry. But I really think you should go back and wait things out," Mr. Mond said. "We have medical supplies and all sorts of great treatments back in the underground base."

"He's right, Viv," Elijah insisted. "Your arm looks like it hurts pretty bad. And with that cannon busted, I don't think you'd be much help if things with the Roswellians turn ugly."

Elijah's words stung. *Does he not think I can keep up? Even after everything we've been through?*

"Yeah," Charlotte agreed. "You'd be a sitting duck."

"There's no way I'm turning back," Viv vowed, her voice breaking. "You don't have to protect me. I can protect myself. And I'm not leaving here without my mom."

Mr. Mond and Charlotte helped Viv up to her feet. The broken metal pieces of her arm cannon crumbled to the ground.

"Why don't we send her down through the drainpipe where you came in?" Charlotte offered. "She'll be safe there for now."

"Good idea, Charlotte," Mr. Mond agreed.

Viv pulled away from them both. "No!" she shouted. She held her injured arm to her body and plodded a few steps farther into the jungle.

"We're so close!" Viv pleaded. "If we just keep going—"

"Viv."

Elijah's voice caught her off guard. He laid a hand on her shoulder.

Viv whipped around to find his face inches away from hers. He stared back at her with a sweet, understanding smile.

She looked out at her friends gathered there. Elijah.

Charlotte. Ray. They'd all been through so much, and she knew they only wanted the best for her.

But this time, they're wrong.

"Then I'll go alone," Viv declared.

She brushed Elijah's hand off her shoulder and turned away.

"Viv, hold on," Elijah begged. "Let's talk about this!"

All at once, the twilight coming in through the treetops turned to darkness as a huge shadow passed overhead. Only one Roswellian was big enough to block out that much light.

"Megdar . . . ," Viv growled.

She squinted up toward the canopy. Through the cracks in the leaves and pines, she saw his familiar horrific shape hover by. Smaller Roswellians flanked him as they went.

One of his massive tentacles was wrapped around something. A tuft of black, curly hair with silver strands peeked out from his grip.

A knot formed in the pit of Viv's stomach.

Mom.

Megdar paraded her around to the other Roswellians, showing off her unconscious body like a trophy.

A surge of rage rushed through Viv. The pain she felt in her arm dissolved. Her tears dried in an instant. She knew what she had to do.

"Wait!" Elijah called out. "Stop!"

But it was no use. Viv dashed off into the jungle.

Alone.

CHAPTER NINETEEN

Viv ran as fast as she could. The voices of her friends and Mr. Mond rang out through the trees behind her. Pine needles stung the exposed skin on her arm.

She dashed below the aliens' trail in the air, following Megdar step by step as he zoomed through the sky. Had the canopy of trees not been so thick, the monstrous alien king easily could have spotted her from above.

But at this point, Viv didn't really care. Her mom was so close, and Viv wasn't going to let her go again without a fight.

Two pine trees dipped into her path. Viv reached out with her good arm to separate them and ducked below the wide branches.

Suddenly, the ground switched from crunchy leaves to hard white concrete.

The center of the terrarium.

Viv stood at the edge of the big blank circle. All the wedges of the sectors met here. It looked like the center of a huge pizza pie—each slice a different flavor of terrain.

Viv craned her neck and glared up toward the sky. The glistening Roswellian spaceship hovered just below the porthole exit, nearly two hundred feet in the air.

The core of the ship was a solid steel compartment shaped like a sphere. Halos of long, thick metal revolved around the center. Each shimmering ring rotated on a different axis, creating a mesmerizing effect. It reminded Viv of the gyroscope her physics teacher used to keep on her desk.

Charlotte and Elijah caught up to her first. Ray and Mr. Mond followed a few paces behind.

They pulled Viv back into the cover of the trees. "Viv!" Charlotte chided. "What are you *doing*? Your arm is hurt. We need to get you back to . . ."

Charlotte's concern faded away to nothing in Viv's ears. Viv was more focused on a bigger problem. She peered back out, examining the bottom of the sphere core.

A massive fuel tank made up the lower portion of the ship's solid center. The hatch that opened into the tank had two metal doors made of pointed steel. Each cut of steel jutted out like a sharp knife, and the hatch doors slammed open and closed over and over again. Inside, a burning hot furnace blazed. It looked like two huge metal jaws chewing in a heavy rhythm.

Dozens of Roswellian soldiers flew back and forth between the ship and the different terrarium sectors, pulling up trees from the ground with their telekinetic powers and tossing them into the fuel tank, prepping for takeoff. The steel doors crunched through the thick pine trees like they were toothpicks.

A familiar, dark shadow passed over Viv's line of sight once again.

Megdar zoomed up to the top of the ship and dropped Director Harlow into the spherical core. Her unconscious body narrowly missed the fast-moving gyrating rings.

Viv clenched her fist and whipped around to face her friends.

"You're the only one who can get up that high, Elijah," Viv said, talking over Charlotte's concerns for her arm. "You need to fly up to the top and scout the layout of the ship."

Elijah looked rapidly back and forth between Viv and Charlotte, clearly unsure who to listen to. With the monstrous spaceship just above them, the danger had became very real once more, and despite her hurt arm, Viv was still another number against the horde.

"Elijah." Viv's voice turned urgent. "We have to do this now. We're running out of time before they take off with all our parents."

Elijah tore his gaze away and refused to make eye contact. She could see him biting his lip hard enough to leave marks.

Viv laid her hand on his shoulder. Normally, the thought of touching him would make her want to faint. But the intensity of the moment had taken over, and for once she knew exactly what to say to him.

"Your dad needs you," Viv urged. "We all need you."

Charlotte's gaze softened. Ray gave Meekee a tight squeeze of comfort. Even Mr. Mond seemed moved.

Elijah finally nodded. "You're right," he said. "We can do this."

Viv smiled. That was the Elijah she knew.

"When you get up there, radio us on your wrist communicator and tell us what you see," Viv directed. "Be careful. And remember, once you're above them, they won't be able to see you."

Elijah nodded once more before extending the wings on his flight suit and clicking his heels together. The engine sputtered to life and chugged him up into the air. Running low on fuel, he was slower than usual, but he climbed steadily until he soared above the trees.

"What do we do now?" Ray asked.

Viv glanced around the circle; the nervous energy among them was palpable. Charlotte's gauntlets sparkled under the thin rays of twilight pouring in through the porthole as she paced back and forth. Mr. Mond propped the O.D.O.R. on a mossy rock, tinkering nervously with the plastic barrel. Ray cradled Meekee in the palm of his hand, petting him half-heartedly.

Viv knew this was it. Their last chance to stop Megdar and his army. Her last chance to save everyone.

My last chance to save Mom.

She closed her eyes. They needed a strategy.

A battle plan.

Different possibilities swirled through her head. One wrong step, and she and her friends would be captured, just as helpless as the others.

The screen on her wrist communicator lit up. A long crack ran through the glass, and it seemed like the hologram feature was broken, but Elijah's voice came in clear.

"Viv. Come in, Viv."

Everyone crowded around the fractured communicator on Viv's sleeve. "We can hear you, Elijah," she called back.

"I'm above their line of sight," Elijah said. "The Roswellians are loading up the last of the hostages. Looks like they're almost ready for takeoff.

"Our parents . . ." He trailed off. "They're floating in the cargo hold. They're all in there, along with the rest of the kids."

Viv stared down at her hands and where the bruising on her arm was starting to show. She tried to clear her head, but the rhythmic clanging of the chomping fuel tank clouded her thoughts.

Then, all at once, it hit her. Each move played out in her head like a chess game.

Viv hatched a plan.

Her head snapped up. "Charlotte, how much more of that antigravity gum do you have?"

"Uhh, let me see," Charlotte muttered. She dug into her pocket and pulled out the small purple packet to count.

"Two sticks," Charlotte reported. "Why?"

"Do you think that's enough to flip the ship?" Viv asked.

"Flip the ship! Are you kidding?"

"It worked on the recycling bin, right?" Viv said. "If the atoms of an object touch a piece of the chewed gum, it'll flip the magnetic poles of that object, right?"

"I mean, yeah, I guess so."

"Great," Viv responded. "Then give me the gum."

Charlotte passed her the pack with a shrug.

"Can you create a distraction?"

Charlotte smiled mischievously and held up her gauntlets. "I think I might have some friends who can make some noise."

Viv pressed the button on her wrist communicator. "Elijah, do you think you have enough fuel to take me up to the ship?"

It was quiet for a moment. Then Elijah's voice crackled back in.

"Yes," Elijah said. "I think I have enough for one more trip."

"Perfect."

"How about me? Is there anything I can do?" Mr. Mond asked. "The O.D.O.R. *is* pretty powerful, you know."

"You mean the fart gun?"

"It's not a fart gun!"

"Do the Roswellians even have noses?" Charlotte wondered aloud.

"That's what I said!" Ray chimed in. "Depends on whether they sneeze!"

"Mr. Mond, you cover us from the ground, especially if any more dinosaurs rear their ugly heads," Viv decided. "Only use that thing if we're in immediate danger. I don't want you accidentally knocking yourself or anyone else out with the stink."

"What about me? What can I do?" Ray asked.

"Do you still have that growth ray?"

Ray patted the waistband of his underwear and pulled out the small blue gun.

"Yeah, and last time he used it, he turned himself into a Tater Tot and left us stranded!" Charlotte pointed out.

"Yeah, but I know how to use it now," Ray said indignantly.

"I believe you, Ray," Viv said. "You're the most important part of this."

He squared his shoulders and gave her a thumbs-up.

For the first time throughout this whole ordeal, Viv finally felt confidence bubbling under the surface. All the pieces of the puzzle were falling into place.

"If we stay stealthy and everyone sticks to the plan, I think we can—"

Viv froze.

Megdar.

This time, he was closer overhead than before. The ends of his tentacles scraped the top of the pine trees.

Viv, Charlotte, Ray, and Mr. Mond dove deeper into the jungle. They scrambled and hid under a massive palm frond.

Megdar descended over their hideout. He rambled back

and forth, swaying only a few yards above the brush.

He's looking for something.

"Why don't we just take him out now?" Ray whispered under his breath. "Nobody else has to get hurt. We can end this right now."

He spoke with a confidence Viv had never heard in him before. He was still riding high from his *T. rex* takedown.

"I can hit him." Ray pulled another sonic grenade from his pocket and pawed at the safety pin. "I know I can!"

"Ray, wait! No!" Viv shouted.

Ray tossed the grenade into the air with the same follow-through as his shot at the *T. rex*. This time, his aim wasn't quite as lucky.

The grenade arched over the palm frond and whizzed by Megdar's left side. It hit a tree branch and bounced back down to the jungle floor.

Sound exploded through the terrarium. The wormhole ripped open, sucking in a massive pine tree before dissolving into thin air.

Megdar whipped around in the group's direction.

They'd been seen. It was too late.

Megdar's body glowed bright green. Within seconds, a terrifying army of Roswellians zoomed down through the treetops at lightning speed.

Directly toward Viv and her friends.

CHAPTER TWENTY

The horde of Roswellians descended on them like a swarm of locusts. The tiny sliver of twilight that spilled in from the porthole was darkened by their shadows.

"Nice distraction, Ray!" Charlotte yelled, sarcasm coating every syllable.

"I'm sorry, guys!"

Charlotte took a deep breath and clenched her fists inside her gauntlets. Duplicates flooded into the sky. Hundreds of copies of Charlotte charged toward the alien mob in their own equally impressive formation.

The clones crashed into the first line of Roswellians, slamming them with a fury of punches and kicks.

Mr. Mond stepped in front of Charlotte, shielding her from danger as she commanded her army of clones. He fired the O.D.O.R. skyward, sending a colossal fog of toxic green fumes into the air.

The Roswellians slowed to a halt. One by one, each alien

that flew into the cloud of fart sneezed and then dropped out of the sky.

"I TOLD you they have nostrils!" Mr. Mond yelled.

His and Charlotte's defenses had bought the rest of them some time. Viv turned to Ray, grabbed his wrists, and spoke quickly. "Ray, I need you to get directly under the spaceship and have the growth ray ready."

"Now?" Ray gulped.

"NOW!" Viv shouted.

Ray took off as fast as his legs could carry him. He ducked under the jungle brush and sprinted out onto the blank circle in the center of the terrarium.

Even though Charlotte and Mr. Mond had managed to subdue dozens of Roswellians, the back lines of the swarm still advanced. There were just too many of them.

Viv slammed the button on her tattered wrist communicator. "Elijah!" she hollered. "Come back! We're under atta—"

"Already on it!"

Elijah's voice rang out loud and clear. But this time it wasn't coming from the communicator.

It was coming from right behind her.

Elijah swooped down from the treetops and picked Viv up, literally sweeping her off her feet.

Before she knew it, she was soaring through the air. She could see everything from above. Elijah turned his wings around the Roswellian horde, skimming along the outer flanks of their formation. He focused straight ahead, navigating them through each stray tentacle that jutted from the alien army like an expert pilot.

Elijah bent their flight path around the last line of the aliens, and they shot out of the other end and into clear skies. The engine chugged along at his back. Only a few yards separated them and the alien ship.

Despite the chaos surrounding them, Viv couldn't help but notice how the dusky light shone down from the porthole onto Elijah's face, twinkling off the dark brown waves in his hair. His cheeks were bright red from the adrenaline, but he managed to shoot her a quick smile. If their parents hadn't been on the brink of intergalactic abduction, it would have been a pretty romantic moment . . .

One of the revolving halos surrounding the ship whizzed by Elijah and Viv, almost knocking them out of the sky. Elijah banked hard and pulled them away from the danger.

"Stop here!" Viv called to Elijah.

They hovered just outside the halo's reach, blocked by the outline of the ship. The alien army couldn't see them from this position, leaving them safe for the moment.

Viv patted the pocket of her combat suit, checking that the two sticks of antigravity gum were still safely stowed away.

Yes. Still here. Phew.

She pulled them out and held them at the ready with her uninjured arm, before examining the enemy spacecraft.

The sharp teeth of the fuel tank opened and closed in a rhythmic pattern. Every other second, they slammed open. Every three seconds, one of the gyrating rings swung by the entrance to the fuel tank.

Viv counted over and over in her head. She had to time it perfectly. If her toss was even half a second off, the gum would bounce off the steel and plummet to the ground.

This was it. The centerpiece of her entire plan hinged on this throw.

Viv steadied herself, squeezing the gum tightly in her fist. The muscles in her arm twitched from exhaustion. She closed her eyes, letting the count in her mind fall in line with the rhythm of the ship.

Three . . . two . . . one!

With a powerful sling of her arm, Viv launched the gum through the air.

One stick flew ahead of the other. It slammed into one of the revolving halo rings and rocketed off toward the ground.

The second stick disappeared behind the gyrating rings and into the fuel tank. The metallic teeth sliced through the stick and swallowed it up with a heavy chomp.

I did it!

For a long moment, nothing happened. Then the gyroscope's revolving rings clanged to a halt. After a split second, they started spinning the opposite direction.

FWHOOM!

"Yes!" Elijah cheered. "It worked!"

In one surging whoosh, the entire ship flipped upside down.

The gust of wind knocked Elijah and Viv backward through the air. Elijah leveled them out just in time for Viv to see her plan in action.

The open cargo hold of the ship's sphere tilted toward the ground. The floating contents rattled around.

Then gravity took over.

The pile of unconscious Area 51 employees and their children plunged toward the earth, free-falling with incredible speed.

Viv's eyes shot to the ground, where she could see an ant-size boy shivering in the center of the terrarium's blank circular center.

"RAY!" Viv shouted to the floor, praying he could hear her. The tiny boy's head snapped up at the sound of her voice.

"NOW!"

There was a beat. The figures kept falling, Elijah's engine kept puttering, and all Viv could do was hope with all her heart that Ray would pull through.

Come on, Ray! It's up to you!

Then—from far below she saw the tiniest zap of an electric blue shock.

Immediately, Ray transformed, growing fifty feet tall in the blink of an eye.

He stuck out his jumbo arms and gargantuan hands, catching the falling humans in the nick of time. They snored peacefully in his gigantic palms like a bunch of sleeping babies, oblivious to the danger they'd just been in. Viv frantically scanned the group for her mother, till she saw her nestled in between Charlotte's drooling dad and a fidgety Mr. Yates.

They were safe.

"Yes!" Viv shouted. "Ray! You DID it!"

"You big, beautiful nerd!" Elijah hollered.

Ray peered down in disbelief at all of the lives he'd just saved, cradled in his arms. Then he stared up at Elijah and Viv hovering near the terrarium's glass ceiling.

"WOO-HOO!" Ray shouted. "I'm finally TALL!"

Elijah and Viv shared a weary smile.

But a thunderous sound buzzed from behind and cut their small moment of celebration short.

It was Megdar. Watching his prized human collection fall out of his ship was the last straw. And now he blazed toward Viv and Elijah for revenge, zooming past any other Roswellians that stood in his way.

Elijah's lightning-fast reflexes kicked in. He swerved his flight suit around the ship, narrowly avoiding the whip of Megdar's tentacle.

They circled the ship in a cat-and-mouse chase. But Megdar was faster than the flight suit, making it only a matter of time before he caught up with them.

The fuel gauge on Elijah's wrist rang out in five short beeps. The engine on his back puttered out into frantic bursts.

"Shoot! We're out of fuel!" Elijah shouted. With one final surge, the flight suit jerked forward before starting to fall toward the ground.

With a grunt, Elijah flung Viv high into the air to give her a few extra seconds of hang time before the inevitable descent, and then began to plummet himself.

"NO!" Viv yelled.

Time slowed down.

Viv peered at the expanse that spread out beneath her. Elijah's body tumbled through the air below. His limbs flailed as he tried to fight the gravity pulling him to the terrarium floor.

Viv reached out toward the ground, feeling helpless as she watched Elijah plummet below her. She could sense herself falling, too, but like everything else around her, it seemed like slow motion.

Tears welled in her eyes. Her heart felt like it was being ripped in two.

A strange green glow built up around her outstretched injured arm.

She felt the pull of Elijah's body weight in her hand, as if she was holding him up. Her arm throbbed with pain, but something inside her, something *instinctive*, told her to pull. Viv strained her muscles and curled her arms as tight as she could.

Suddenly, Elijah's body was enveloped in the same green glowing light.

My arm . . . Elijah! What's happening?

He was only thirty feet from reaching the ground, about to make impact any second, but the glowing force slowed his descent.

Below, the alien army still swarmed Charlotte and Mr. Mond. Charlotte's gauntlets were falling apart, their knuckles completely scraped and cracking from the battle. The O.D.O.R. was on its last canister of gas. They didn't have much fight left.

In the midst of the battle, Charlotte looked up at just the right moment to notice Elijah's glowing green silhouette still falling through the air.

Viv watched as Charlotte clenched her battered gauntlets to spawn thirty clones in a continuous chain. They immediately formed a human pyramid, allowing the top clone to catch Elijah at the last second and pass him down the chain of clones until he was safely on the ground.

Viv breathed a sigh of relief. The green glow surrounding her arm evaporated to nothing. She closed her eyes, finally feeling time speed up again and the full weight of gravity's pull on her own body take hold. Her hair whipped around her face as she dropped through the air.

A loud buzzing sound closed in on her.

BAM!

Viv felt the breath leave her lungs as Megdar collided with her in midair.

CHAPTER
TWENTY-ONE

Viv and Megdar crashed into one of the steel halos surrounding the ship. Their impact against the metal propelled them up toward the hard glass dome of the terrarium's ceiling.

Like flipping a switch, Megdar's entire body glowed neon green with his telekinetic field as he wrapped Viv up in the force field with him.

Viv shut her eyes. She'd seen what Megdar was capable of when he almost crushed Elijah back in the battle outside the Gadgets Room. She braced herself for the pain . . .

But his telekinetic grip was gentle.

What? Why isn't he hurting me like he did Elijah?

Megdar carried her alongside him, softly propelling her through the air and back down to the ship. Viv felt like she was floating on a fluffy green cloud—a far cry from the terror she felt coursing through her veins.

They rose up through the cargo hold until they reached a large room.

The cockpit.

The interior of the spaceship was all smooth gray steel. A vast control panel stretched around the room with buttons and dials in shapes Viv had never even seen before. Only a long panel of glass windows looked familiar to her. She tried to crane her neck to see if her friends were safe on the ground, but Megdar pulled her back toward the center of the room.

They floated, suspended in the upside-down cabin. Megdar telekinetically pressed a button from across the room, causing a mechanical whirring to spark beneath Viv's feet. A large sheet of steel slid in where there was no floor, isolating them from the terrarium air.

They were completely alone.

Viv gulped. Even though she knew Megdar's telekinetic hold was keeping her in one place, every instinct in her body told her to scream, to run and hide from this monster before it was too late. But then she began to feel a different instinct take hold, as the pit of hatred that had been growing inside her finally boiled over.

"Why don't you just get it over with?" she spat.

"Get *what* over with?" Megdar chuckled. "I'm not going to hurt you, child."

From each of his thousands of eyes, the neon green glow erupted in long beams. Viv shielded her face from the blinding light with the crook of her elbow. She pulled her arm down and examined the spot where the hideous alien creature had been floating just moments ago, only to find Megdar back in his human form.

Even after all of the fighting and chaos of the day, his long khaki trench coat was pristine, not a wrinkle in sight. Viv knew his true alien form still lurked beneath the surface, yet somehow, being trapped in a tiny room with his human version made her feel slightly more at ease. In his human form, at least she stood a chance against him.

"You and your friends . . . you're valiant," Megdar admitted. "I'm impressed you made it this far without being captured."

Viv turned her head to stare out the cockpit window again, not dignifying the compliment with a response.

Megdar let out a sigh and tried again.

"What do they call you, child?" Megdar asked, his sinister green eyes glowing bright.

Viv gritted her teeth. She didn't want to tell him, but there was no point in lying to him now.

"Viv," she said, seething. "Vivian Harlow."

"Vivian *Harlow* . . ." Megdar laughed.

"What's so funny?" Viv snapped.

"That last name has caused me more trouble than you know."

"Let me guess . . . You know my mom?"

"Yes." He scowled. "I'm sad to say that I do."

Viv puffed up her chest. "Hey! My mother is a great woman!

You just don't like her because she's not afraid of you! From the looks of it, she scares YOU!"

Megdar lurched toward her. Viv instinctively tried to jump back, but the telekinetic field holding her in place made it impossible. She was trapped in her own body as Megdar swooped in close, a vulture hovering above its prey.

"Your mother was very clever," Megdar whispered. "Years ago, she showed me kindness when I thought your planet had none."

Megdar tilted the brim of his hat below his eyes, casting a long shadow across his face. He let out a deep, almost mournful sigh.

"It wasn't until later that I realized she had used me. Just like the rest of your deceitful species," he growled.

Viv felt a shiver tremble down her spine. Even though Megdar said he wouldn't hurt her, he obviously held a deep grudge against her mom, and who knew what he would do with Viv to get to Director Harlow. She couldn't let panic take hold now. She had to be logical here.

How can I convince him to let me go?

"You don't have to do this," Viv said, hoping that pity would be her savior. "You and the Roswellians can still leave this planet in peace."

"Roswellians?" Megdar scoffed. "That horrible name was given to us by our captors. We only use it because our real name cannot be pronounced in your language."

"Try me," Viv challenged.

"Jioaefvuhnspibvaqesoiphezysnuxeshbaciojefgijvslegj-sbnetposemajpihogvusb."

"Okay, you may be right."

Megdar grinned. He floated over to the glass panel and stared out at the night sky above, pacing back and forth in midair.

"When our people crash-landed here all those decades ago, we were greeted peacefully by members of the human race. Our ship was in bad shape, and they offered to help us rebuild so we could be on our way. Everything was going smoothly . . . until we needed the final steel panel placed back on the ship. The metal piece was too large and too heavy for the human machinery to lift. So foolishly, I lifted the steel with what you would call telekinesis. When the humans learned that our species possessed this gift, they wanted us to reveal the secret. When we refused and fought back to hold on to our birthright, we became their prisoners. They locked us away deep within this horrible place and separated me from my people, weakening our powers and our spirits."

His voice swelled with emotion. "I made the mistake of revealing our powers. It's my fault that we were even taken as prisoners in the first place," Megdar explained, wiping his eyes. "Now we just want to go home."

"If you want to go, just go!" Viv replied. "Leave us in peace! Why take hostages with you?"

"That's a good question," he said. "You know, you really are very smart."

Megdar turned his back to Viv. He peered out of the glass window of the cockpit, staring down at his army patiently waiting below.

"I've been a prisoner much longer than you've been alive, Vivian. When you've been locked up for long enough, a hatred grows inside of you. Perhaps part of me wanted to see my captors taken captive themselves."

He strode back and forth, seeming to consider his next words carefully.

"But honestly, the better part of me doesn't care about taking any of *those* people."

He motioned toward the employees of Area 51 on the terrarium floor beneath his feet. "We only needed them to find what was stolen from us. To draw the progeny out of hiding."

Viv stared out of the window, peering down at her friends gathered on the ground below. Ray had reverted to his normal size. The tiniest speck of green poked out of his shirt pocket.

Viv suddenly remembered her last bargaining chip.

Meekee.

"I can get you the progeny!" Viv offered. "Just let me go back down to my friends, and I'll bring ba—"

"We already have what was stolen from us," he said. "And it's here on this ship . . . *right now.*"

Viv felt her skin start to crawl.

"It was your mother, you know," Megdar insisted. "Cassandra's the one who stole our powers to use for her research. To create a progeny as a weapon for your planet."

Viv moved toward him as far as the telekinetic hold would let her. Hearing her mother's name come out of this creature's mouth filled her with fury.

"Whatever she did, maybe she was right!" Viv cried. "Look at all the destruction you've caused since you busted out. Maybe she was just trying to protect humans from monsters like you!"

Megdar slammed his fist down onto the control panel. "Do you think I even *want* to be on this horrible planet?!" he howled. He took a deep breath and brushed off his shoulders, momentarily regaining his composure. "Listen, I'm not here to take over your world. And I assure you, I'm not a monster."

"You've destroyed the base, you've hurt people, and you've kidnapped children. Seems like a monster to me!" Viv shouted back.

"I know who I am!" Megdar snarled. "But the question is . . . do you know who you are?"

What? What does he mean?

Viv squirmed against the telekinesis, but he took another step closer. Even in his human form, he was a very tall man, looming over Viv at almost double her size.

"Noticed anything . . . strange lately?" Megdar prompted. "Did something happen that you felt like you couldn't explain?

Something your friends couldn't understand, either?"

Viv shook her head and tried to push his questions from her mind. But it wasn't enough to stop the memories from flooding in.

She thought back to the air vent closing on its own in the main hall. She remembered the mysterious green energy blast she shot at Megdar outside the Gadgets Room, even when her arm cannon was broken. And even just a few moments ago, watching Elijah's body slow down as he fell through the air, like Viv was invisibly pulling him back toward her, even as her own descent was slowed.

No. It can't be. None of that was because of me . . .

"Area 51 is a place full of secrets," Megdar warned. "Don't believe everything you're told."

Viv realized Megdar was standing right beside her now.

"The people who work here are clever. They lie to suit their own purposes."

Megdar curled in behind Viv's ear.

"Sometimes, even to their own daughters . . ."

Viv looked down at her hands. The same faint green glow that blazed in Megdar's eyes emanated from her own arms.

"Vivian . . ." Megdar lowered his voice. "I wasn't positive it was you until I saw you save your friend, but now I know for sure."

Viv didn't want to believe what she was hearing. Her head was spinning. She felt the air leave her lungs.

"*You* are the progeny."

CHAPTER
TWENTY-TWO

THIRTEEN YEARS EARLIER . . .

Cassandra Harlow's heels clacked down the long corridor. Area 51 was buzzing with employees. They popped in and out of the countless experimentation rooms, hastily writing notes on their clipboards.

Though she'd only been working there for a few months, Cassandra felt like she already had a good mental map of the place. Her curly black hair bounced against her shoulders with each step.

She rounded a corner and entered a less populated hallway, where only a few technicians and scientists passed her as she made her way deeper into the compound. A long, grinding escalator took her down four stories into a heavily armed section of the base.

Down here, she was completely alone.

Cassandra craned her neck to read the numbers marked on the doors.

Subsector 411 . . .

Subsector 412 . . .

Aha. Here we go: 413.

She made it. Finally, she'd found the containment cells where Area 51 kept its most dangerous test subjects.

Cassandra swiped her badge against the endless scanners that kept this hallway under extreme lockdown. Each swipe opened up a pair of heavy steel doors. After six swipes, she finally made it to the last door.

She swiped her badge against the scanner marked "6JW." The screen lit up red, flashing the words "ACCESS DENIED" over and over again. She didn't have the clearance to go past this point.

Luckily, she'd prepared for this moment. One week ago, while Director Martinez was giving his monthly briefing to all of the Area 51 employees, Cassandra caught a brief glimpse of the security code around his keychain. Even though it was just for a second, she memorized the sixteen digits printed on the tag and stored it in the back of her mind. She knew it would come in handy eventually.

Cassandra punched in the numbers carefully.

8-9-5-2-3-2-2-5-9-3-8-1-7-4-2-5.

The doors slid open. It worked.

Cassandra stepped inside the surprisingly comfortable observation room. A couch in the corner, a large bathroom, and a mini fridge fully stocked with food and refreshments implied that scientists had spent days at a time down here, giving it the feel of a lounge more than a lab. But on the other side of the thick bulletproof glass window, the holding tank wasn't quite so cozy.

Megdar was restrained on the other side of the glass. He was in his grotesque alien form, looking ragged and exhausted. His appearance sent a shiver down Cassandra's spine, though she was careful not to let it show. She didn't know too much about him, only that he was the leader of an alien race codenamed the Roswellians from planet ZR-18, he had led the aliens in a vicious attack that had injured countless Area 51 agents, and he'd been the subject of dozens of failed experiments to extract his DNA, specifically, his DNA while in his human form. Though they'd managed to get samples from other Roswellians and samples of Megdar in his alien form, the scientists at the compound hadn't managed to transfer his abilities over to humans. They had soon realized that Megdar, as the leader of the alien race, possessed a specific genetic component that was vital to unlocking the telekinetic abilities. They still weren't entirely sure why this was, but much like a queen bee has unique qualities as compared to her worker bees, he was the key to it all. Area 51 agents had been trying to uncover the secrets of his genetic code for decades. But no one had even come close . . . *yet*.

His tentacles dangled above him. The cuffs around each of his appendages pressed tightly into his green skin and a large belt held his core against the steel beam behind his body. His head hung low. He didn't even bother to look up with any of his thousands of eyes when the doors of the observation room opened. At this point, he was used to being watched.

Cassandra took a deep breath and stepped in closer.

"What will it be today?" Megdar groaned.

His voice caught her off guard.

"Brain sensors? Intelligence testing?" Megdar hissed. "I hope they didn't send you down here to try poking me with a needle."

"I'm not here to do any of that," Cassandra replied. "I'm only here to talk. Merely collecting data."

Megdar's many eyes squinted, reading the name badge pinned to Cassandra's lab coat. "Sure," he scoffed. "Whatever you say . . . Agent Harlow."

"Please, call me Cassandra."

She paced back and forth along the glass, examining the weary alien creature in front of her.

"You know, you're the first alien resident of Area 51 that I've spoken with in person," Cassandra said.

"Resident?" Megdar spat. "Ha! We're nothing more than your lab rats."

"Well, I know it's not the Hilton, but it could be much worse," she mused. "I'll be sure to put a mint on your pillow next time I come in."

She chuckled and sat down in the chair nearest to the

small, mail-slot opening in the glass where the technicians pushed food in each day.

"Who sent you?" Megdar asked. "Let me guess. From the looks of you, I'd say the Weapons Department."

"No one sent me," Cassandra emphasized. "Actually, I'm not even supposed to be in here. Promise you won't tell my boss?"

Megdar focused his eyes on her for the first time before quickly averting them back toward the floor. "I don't know if the others have told you, but I'm not the easiest test subject to deal with."

"Oh, I've heard the stories," Cassandra said. "I heard they sent Agent Becker down here last week to try to take a DNA sample. He still can't move his arm after what you did to him."

Megdar grew quiet. His tentacles curled in.

"I didn't know that I'd injured him that badly," Megdar confessed with guilt in his voice. "It was never my intention."

"That's okay," she said. "I never really liked him, anyway."

Megdar let out a burst of laughter, tentacles unfurling in response, as if her frankness had surprised it out of him.

"I'm surprised you're not more . . . disturbed by me," Megdar grumbled. "The appearance of our species is somewhat off-putting to humans."

"Oh, I'm not easily scared. Believe me, I've dated guys that look worse."

She flashed him a smile, and Megdar hesitantly chuckled

back. She felt emboldened—clearly, she was starting to make an impression.

Cassandra pressed on. "Although you're welcome to change into your human form whenever you'd like."

Megdar eyed her suspiciously, and his laughter instantly stopped. "Even if I wanted to, these constraints block my power."

"Well, I'm sure there's something we can do about that."

She stood up from her chair and walked back toward the control panel against the observation desk. She entered in the same sixteen-digit code and hit a button marked "Release."

The cuffs around Megdar's tentacles immediately snapped open. Cassandra could practically see the wave of relief run through him as he was able to stretch his limbs for the first time in decades. He rubbed his raw squid-wrists, careful to avoid the indents in his skin from the squeezing pressure.

"There you go," Cassandra said. "That should be more comfortable."

She turned toward the table by the mini fridge, where a teakettle was tucked away among stacks of overflowing paper. Cassandra sorted through the mess and pulled the teakettle over to the sink in the bathroom. She filled it with water and set it down on top of the single Bunsen burner in the room, usually reserved for heating up chemicals.

"I can only imagine how badly you want to go home," Cassandra said over her shoulder. "From reading your records, you've been in this sector quite a long time."

"Just let me see my people," Megdar pleaded. "It's not fair to keep me separated from them. They need me."

"You know I can't do that," Cassandra sighed. "But if you help me, I can make sure that *all of you* can go home. Your telekinetic abilities could save millions of human lives. I have so many ideas of how we can improve the planet with these abilities. All you need to do is teach us how to harness them."

"My people and I are not interested in teaching any of our gifts, our birthright," Megdar objected. "You humans are only interested in destruction. Even if we were to gift you this knowledge, you would learn the wrong lesson."

Cassandra returned to the chair by the glass window and leaned in close.

"Can't you see?" Cassandra bargained. "I'm trying to *help* you."

"The humans who captured us in 1947 said the same thing."

"All we need is one measly DNA sample. That's it. Then you can leave."

"There will always be another reason for you people to keep us here."

The teakettle began to whistle.

"Do you really want to spend the rest of your life here?" Cassandra implored.

"My species doesn't age the same way humans do. We could live for thousands of years, even in conditions like this,"

Megdar said. "I will certainly outlast you, and most likely humanity as well."

The teakettle screeched, sending a chill up Cassandra's spine.

She snapped up from her seat and walked over to the Bunsen burner. She carefully lifted the kettle off the flame and pulled two mugs and two tea bags out of the overhead cabinet. She dropped the a bag into each mug with a splash.

The scent of chamomile wafted through the air.

"Mm. That smells good," Megdar admitted.

"You can smell that? All the way from in there?" Cassandra asked.

"Yes—scent is one of my species' strongest senses," Megdar explained.

Cassandra scribbled that note down in her lab book. She picked up one of the mugs and took a long sip.

"Would you like some?" Cassandra said, extending her mug toward the glass. "I bet you've never had tea from Earth before. It's actually pretty good. Supposed to have a calming effect."

Megdar's eyes all stared at her in disbelief. Cassandra hid her smile with another sip of tea. She knew no agent had ever offered him anything apart from the protein paste they fed him to keep him alive.

"I . . . I can't drink liquids in this form," Megdar said. "I'd have to change."

"Well, how 'bout it? I'll loosen that last restraint if you come over here and have a cup of tea with me as a human," Cassandra proposed. "But you have to promise to behave yourself."

"Me? Do you promise to behave *yourself*?" Megdar retorted. "No sneak attacks?"

Cassandra put her hands up and shook her head.

"No sneak attacks here. See? I'll even roll up my sleeves," she promised. "I've got nothing to hide."

She smiled and sauntered to the control panel. She entered the access code, and the restraint holding Megdar's body unlatched with a clunk.

It was the first time he'd been able to move freely in ages, and Megdar gladly stretched out his whole body. He looked back to Cassandra with a hint of gratitude in his thousands of beady eyes. After a few moments, an explosion of green light erupted from beyond the glass. For the first time in over half a century, Megdar changed back into his human form.

Cassandra beamed as he cautiously approached the glass, unsteady on only two feet after so long.

"Well, what do you know? You're not nearly as ugly as people say," Cassandra teased.

Megdar let out a chuckle. His glowing green eyes pierced the inches of bulletproof glass that separated him from the peculiar woman. Cassandra couldn't help but stare.

"There's still so much that we can learn from your people," Cassandra admitted.

The tiny smile was wiped clean from Megdar's face, and the room grew quiet. He stared at her with a delicate patience.

"I plan on being the director of this place one day, you know," Cassandra said.

"Oh, I'm sure you will," Megdar said. "You certainly seem like the most capable person I've met so far."

"When that day comes, I'll be sure you're treated correctly. I hate knowing you and your people are in pain."

"If there's one thing I've learned during my time here, it's that human promises are meaningless."

Cassandra let out a long sigh. She realized her attempts were useless—he was never going to willingly help them.

Cassandra lifted the second mug off the table and blew lightly on the edge of the ceramic. "I hope it's not too hot."

She lifted the small door and slid the mug through the food slot. The steam from the tea fogged up the sides of the opening.

Instead of reaching, Megdar's eyes beamed with electric green light. The mug began glowing the same neon color. Using only his mind, he lifted the mug into the air and caught it with his hand.

"Incredible . . . ," Cassandra whispered, staring in awe at the magic unfolding before her eyes.

Megdar took a long, greedy sip of the tea. "Ahh, that *is* good."

He raised his mug toward her, as if to say thank you. She

smiled and did the same. They each sipped their tea in a comfortable silence until both mugs were empty.

With an almost forlorn look at the empty mug, Megdar passed it back through the slot. Cassandra quickly grabbed the empty cup and pulled it through the glass opening, being sure to securely shut the glass door.

Wordlessly, Cassandra walked over to the observation table and opened a drawer, doing her best to keep her bubbling excitement in check. She reached in and pulled a long cotton swab from deep within the desk. She unscrewed the sterilizing cap and swiped the tip of the swab along the top of Megdar's mug where his lips—and saliva—had left their mark.

"What are you doing?" Megdar asked, his voice turning frantic.

"Like I said, I'm collecting data," Cassandra said plainly. "Did you know that these days you can collect DNA from saliva, and not just blood? We've come a long way since the 1950s. One way or another, I was going to get a sample of your human DNA. And clearly our more . . . aggressive approaches haven't worked."

She put the swab into a plastic bag and secured it in the pocket of her lab coat.

"No! No! You can't take that!" Megdar shouted.

"I am sincerely sorry, Megdar," Cassandra said. "But you have my word—this DNA will be used to save lives, to *create* life, not as a weapon. And when I become director, I *will* make good on my promise to release you and your people."

She entered the access code on the control panel and pressed a button.

Like a magnetic pull, Megdar's body flew backward through the holding tank and into the steel beam. The constraints retightened around his wrists and torso. Anger quickly spread across his face.

He'd been fooled.

"You TRICKED me!" Megdar screamed. "You're just like the rest of them!"

Cassandra turned away from him and headed back toward the door.

"I assure you," Cassandra declared, "I'm not like the others. I'll be back to set you free one day. Once we've learned all we can from your species."

She waved her hand behind her head. The door to the observation room slammed shut behind her.

Through the thick titanium, she could still hear Megdar's screams.

Cassandra smiled to herself as she walked out of the room, knowing that she was on the verge of a major scientific breakthrough. Though hearing the pain in Megdar's voice did give her a stab of guilt, she knew the ends would ultimately justify the means. She left with the DNA sample that countless other agents had failed to obtain . . . and everything she needed to inject herself with the Roswellians' powers.

CHAPTER
TWENTY-THREE

Viv's head was spinning. She felt like she was going to faint, and her knees buckled beneath her. She cupped her hands over her ears, trying not to let Megdar's story break into her mind. Megdar reached out his hand and caught her in his telekinetic grip just before she fell.

She craned her neck up, meeting Megdar's gaze. She searched his bright green eyes for any sign of doubt. She found none.

"No! You're lying!" Viv shouted. "This is a sick joke! One of your alien mind games!"

"I'm sorry, Vivian. But it's true," Megdar consoled her. "It was your mother. She stole my DNA and injected it into herself."

"But why? Why would she do that?" Viv cried.

"She wanted my powers. The Roswellian power." He moved in closer. "But she didn't get them. Instead, they went to you."

I don't understand. I don't understand any of this!

Viv ran shaky fingers through her hair. Her injured arm felt almost numb now. The throbbing in her head had taken over.

"Unbeknownst to Cassandra, she was pregnant at the time, Vivian." Megdar continued. "You were the one who absorbed our Roswellian abilities."

Viv shook her head over and over. "No!" Viv yelled. "You're wrong!"

"You became her lab experiment," Megdar confessed. "Just like I was."

No. That can't be true!

"In our species, powers awaken around the twelfth year of life, and when they did, I could sense your presence. Until then, I hadn't put together exactly how your mother had used my stolen DNA. Today, as you stepped onto the base and I felt your dormant powers echo in me, I knew exactly in that moment that my progeny had returned. And so today, the plan finally came together."

"The plan? What do you mean? You've been *planning* this all along?"

"Yes. Of course. Why else do you think we lured you here with Take Your Kids to Work Day?" Megdar laughed. "Even your mother didn't figure that one out."

"*We?*"

Megdar's face twisted into a peculiar smirk. "How do you think I know all of your mother's secrets? Like I said . . . not everyone who works here is honest."

"But my mom would never lie to me!" Viv fought back.

"I've already told you—your mom is capable of a lot more than you think," Megdar disputed. "She went behind everyone's back and conducted an illegal experiment: mixing the DNA she stole from me with her own . . . or more accurately, mixing it unwittingly with that of her unborn child."

Viv's throat tightened. She tried to protest, but she was too light-headed to get any words out.

"Even your father was against Cassandra injecting herself," Megdar admitted.

Viv's stomach twisted into knots. It was all too much. This alien beast somehow knew more about her own family than Viv did. She mustered up the strength and looked up at Megdar.

"You knew my *father*?" Viv murmured. "How—how do you know all of this?"

"I told you—a convenient twist of fate brought the perfect messenger right to my doorstep. Someone who was more than happy to reveal all this and more to me, for the chance to join us on our journey. I do feel bad that I won't be able to keep up my end of the bargain, but I've learned my lesson about trusting a human."

Megdar heaved a heavy sigh.

"We can talk about all of this later," he said, turning his back to Viv as he floated over to the ship's upside-down control panel.

"Later?" Viv asked.

"Yes," Megdar replied. "Vivian . . ." He turned back toward her, leaning in close. His eyes burned luminescent green. "I'm not leaving this planet without you."

Viv's breath caught in her chest. It all made sense now. He didn't want Meekee.

He was after me.

"A human child born with our abilities? It would be careless of me to leave you behind on a planet that is not ready for your potential," Megdar insisted. "You belong with us. We can help you hone your powers. We can help you learn who you truly are."

Megdar fidgeted with switches on the control panel, preparing the ship for takeoff. Viv scrunched her eyes up tight.

No. This can't be happening. This is all a bad dream! Wake up! Wake up!

Viv opened her eyes. But nothing had changed. Megdar still fiddled with the control panel, and the spaceship still glowed around her. The nightmare was all too real.

"Without proper guidance and proper lessons, your power could spin out of control. You could end up hurting the people you care about," Megdar continued, oblivious to Viv's inner turmoil.

Viv felt her vision starting to blur. Her mind flashed back to the battle in the hallway . . . when she shot that green energy blast toward the ceiling that freed Elijah from Megdar's clutches . . . but injured him in the process.

She could picture the burn mark on Elijah's side.

The mark that I *caused.*

The memory sparked Viv's rage. She reached out and grabbed Megdar's trench coat in a balled-up fist.

"I'll NEVER hurt anyone!" Viv cried. "Not EVER again!"

"You might not mean to," Megdar said almost kindly. "But your powers become stronger when you're angrier. Like right now."

His eyes motioned down to where Viv was holding his coat. She gazed down, too.

Her hand glowed bright green.

No!

She snapped her arm away and frantically shook it, as if she could shake the glow from her hand like pesky drops of water.

"You'll never be able to understand your powers on your own, Vivian. Even stubbing your toe has the potential to send you into a destructive meltdown."

"My friends wouldn't let that happen!" Viv said. "They would understand. They would help me!"

But Viv grew quiet, the rage starting to subside. The reality of her situation was starting to set in. She imagined what it would be like explaining to her friends that she had alien DNA running through her veins.

How could I even tell them?

"Do you really want them to know?" Megdar asked, as if reading her mind. "Think about it, Vivian. If they know about you, about who and what you really are . . . your entire life will be different."

"My entire life will be different if I move to *another planet*!" Viv shot back.

Megdar laughed. "That's a good point," he admitted. "You have your mother's sharp sense of humor, you know."

Viv looked down at her hands.

Maybe he's right.

Maybe I am *dangerous.*

She thought about Ray, how scared of her he would be if he knew the truth. She imagined Charlotte and her big mouth, blabbing about it to everyone at school. Her heart hurt just thinking of Elijah.

Would he even still talk to me? If he knew I was a freak?

She'd be an outcast. She thought back to how normal her whole life had been just yesterday at school. Then she remembered why she was so sad in the first place. After this summer, she'd be stranded at a new school with no one who understood her.

All I wanted was one last summer with my friends . . . but now, if they realize I'm a monster . . . what difference would it make?

She looked up at Megdar, who was patiently waiting for her to come to this inevitable conclusion.

"If I agree to go with you . . . you'll leave this planet in peace?" Viv asked.

"Yes," Megdar promised. "You have my word."

Viv took a deep breath and wiped the tears out of her eyes. She knew what she had to do.

"Okay," she said. "I'll go with you."

A wide smile spread across Megdar's face. He cupped both of her shoulders in his hands.

"Excellent," Megdar buzzed. "You've made the right choice. You're a very smart young lady, Vivian. Just as I suspected. I promise you, your new life is just beginning!"

Megdar turned his back to her and continued flipping switches on the control panel.

"Takeoff should be relatively simple. We just need to locate the key to the spaceship, which has gone missing."

"You lost the key?" Viv asked incredulously.

"It's been almost eighty years. Don't blame me," Megdar replied. "Oh, and I don't have a seat that fits your human body form, so we'll have to improvise—"

As Megdar rattled on about the ship's departure plans, Viv peered down through the glass window to the terrarium floor. She could just make out the tiny human shapes on the ground two hundred feet below. The other employees and kids who had been unconscious were finally starting to wake up. Ray, Charlotte, Elijah, and Mr. Mond helped them to their feet.

She caught a glimpse of a familiar streak of gray hair.

Mom.

Viv's hands curled into fists.

She watched as Mr. Yates helped Director Harlow to her feet. Her mom's head snapped up, staring straight toward the ship's window where Viv stood.

Since this whole ordeal had begun, all Viv had wanted was

to be reunited with her mom, with the one person who'd protected her for her entire life.

Could she really have been lying to me all this time?

"Vivian," Megdar cooed. "Look."

He placed a hand on her shoulder and pointed toward Viv's reflection in the glass window.

"Your eyes."

Viv glared at her reflection. Her eyes were normally green, but now they gleamed with an inner neon light.

Viv had always wondered how she ended up with green eyes. Her mom's eyes were a deep chocolate brown, so Viv had assumed that her father's eyes were green.

Now she knew the truth.

It was true.

All of it was true.

Viv closed her eyes. She accepted her fate.

She pressed the button on her wrist communicator. "Elijah? Are you there?" Viv called out. "Can you hear me?"

It took a few seconds for the radio signal to reach the ground. Then—

"Viv!" Elijah's frantic voice crackled in through the beat-up speaker on Viv's wrist. "Are you hurt? I'm coming to get you! When I see that jerk Megdar, I'm gonna—"

"Listen." Viv cut him off before he said anything that could get them both in trouble. "They've agreed to leave Earth peacefully."

"Are you serious? That's amazing!" Elijah said. "But we're

all worried about you down here!"

"Is your dad okay?" Viv asked, trying to steer the conversation away from her.

"He's a little bruised up, but he'll be all right," Elijah said cheerfully. She could hear the relief in his voice even through the speaker.

"All of our parents and the other agents are waking up now," he continued. "Turns out, Charlotte's dad had an extra canister of jet fuel on him. My flight suit will be up and running again in a few minutes, and I'll come get you!"

"Elijah." Viv's voice grew stern. "I'm not coming back."

It was silent for a moment.

"W-what?" Elijah stammered. "What do you mean?"

"Megdar has agreed to leave peacefully . . . ," Viv choked out. "If I go with him."

Just saying it out loud terrified her, but she knew she had to be strong. If sacrificing herself meant keeping her friends safe, she had to do it.

Even if it means keeping them safe from me.

Charlotte's and Ray's voices chirped up from the wrist communicator.

"What? No!" Ray protested.

"Have you lost it?" Charlotte shouted.

"It's the only way!" Viv cried out. "Either he takes me, or he takes all of you. We don't have any other option. It's an easy choice."

"She's right." Megdar cut in, leaning in toward the wrist com. "Let us leave in peace, and I promise we won't harm the girl."

Viv wiped away the tears forming in her eyes. She looked across the horizon, over the dozens of terrarium sectors laid out before her.

An ocean.

A desert.

An icy tundra.

As she stood there, preparing to depart for another planet, Viv realized that she'd never gotten the chance to see the world. But then again, maybe this wasn't such a terrible way to say goodbye to Earth.

"I've made my decision," Viv said.

For a moment, it went silent on the other end.

Viv looked down through the window and saw her friends anxiously huddled on the terrarium floor.

She pressed the button on her communicator. "Elijah?" she whispered.

"Yeah?" His voice trembled.

"Can you do me one last favor?" Viv asked.

He paused for a moment before responding. "Anything," he vowed.

Viv looked to Megdar, who smiled back at her.

"I need you to bring us the key."

CHAPTER
TWENTY-FOUR

"The key? The key to the spaceship?" Ray asked. "How are we supposed to find that?"

Back on the ground, Charlotte and Ray were huddled close around Elijah's wrist communicator, hanging on to Viv's every word.

They both looked to Elijah for an answer. He tried to think of something to say, something heroic that would quell their panic. But instead he felt a tingle behind his eyes. Elijah shoved the feeling down before either of his friends could see the tears welling up.

Charlotte finally spoke instead. "Maybe one of them has it?" she stated, pointing at the army of Roswellians hovering in a circle around them.

Dozens of the massive alien creatures floated patiently, waiting for a signal from their leader to attack in case the humans on the ground decided to fight back again.

A tiny voice peeped up out of Ray's shirt pocket.

"Meekee! Meekee! Meekee!"

"Not now, Meekee!" Ray hushed him and pushed the little alien back into his pocket.

Elijah suddenly jerked straight up. "Wait a second . . . What did he say?"

"What do you *mean*, what did he say?" Ray replied. "The only thing he's been saying this whole time!"

"Look!" Elijah pointed toward Ray's pocket, at the tiny head sticking out.

Meekee's body glowed a bright fluorescent green: the same color as Megdar and the other Roswellians.

"Ray. I need you to give me Meekee," Elijah demanded, sticking out his palm.

"What? Why?" Ray cupped his hand defensively around his tiny alien friend.

"I can't believe I didn't realize this earlier." Elijah took a step toward Ray.

"R-realize what?" Ray asked.

"Like you said, he's been saying it this whole time," Elijah said.

Elijah took another step closer. Ray took a step back.

"Meekee *is* THE KEY!" Elijah explained.

"Meekee! Meekee! Meekee!"

"Oh, duh!" Charlotte chimed in. " 'Me key!' You key!"

"No way! You can't take him!" Ray cried out. "We're— we're friends! Please! I could never have gotten through this without him. I'm totally ready to be his mom now! And his aunt. And his first cousin!"

"I'm sorry, Ray," Elijah apologized. "But we have another friend who needs us. We have to do this for Viv."

Ray looked at Elijah with pleading eyes before his expression gave way to acceptance. Ray slowly nodded and gently pulled Meekee out of the cozy shirt pocket.

"I guess this is goodbye, little buddy," Ray whimpered.

Meekee gazed up at him with big, sad eyes of his own.

"I don't even know if you can understand what I'm saying right now," Ray continued. "But I want you to know that this goodbye is not easy for me. It's very . . . It's very—"

"Meekee!" the little alien chirped back.

"Yes, you're right. It is very Meekee," Ray nodded in agreement, wiping a bit of snot from his nose.

Charlotte stepped in closer to Ray and Meekee. "Hey, where's my goodbye hug?"

With a sniffle, Ray handed Meekee off to Charlotte. She held the little alien in her gauntlet and pulled him into her chest for a tight hug. "Tell Viv I love her, okay?"

"Meekee!" he chirped in response.

Charlotte smiled. She passed Meekee to Elijah, who pulled his friends into a tight hug. They stayed there all together, whispering support to each other under their breath before Elijah finally pulled back and took a few steps to his left.

He perfectly positioned himself under the ship, ready to

take off. Just before he flipped the engine on his suit, a voice called out.

"Don't do it, Elijah."

Director Harlow's voice was fraying but stern. Still regaining her strength, she stepped out from behind Mr. Mond.

"That's my daughter up there," Director Harlow argued. "And if you hand Megdar that key, you'll be a part of this intergalactic kidnapping."

"Viv asked me to do this for her. I trust her," Elijah replied. "She said that this is the only way."

Director Harlow took a few heavy steps toward him.

"She's still my daughter!" she shouted. "We just can't let him take her."

Elijah's dad stepped in between them. "Hold on, Director Harlow," Lieutenant Padilla said. "Let's hear him out."

"No! There's got to be another way," Director Harlow said, turning her focus back to Elijah. "That's my daughter, and this is my compound. When you're in Area 51, the decisions come from one place and one place only. Me. Not you. Not your dad. And not Viv."

"But Viv saved your life!" Elijah whipped around to face all the other employees and their children huddled around him. "Her plan saved ALL of our lives! And now she's about to do it again."

Director Harlow took a deep breath. "At least let me speak to her. Please, Elijah. She's my baby girl."

He looked to his father for direction, and Lieutenant Padilla gave him a nod. Elijah extended his wrist so Director Harlow could speak into the communicator.

She pressed the button and spoke slowly.

"Viv, are you there?" Director Harlow asked. "It's Mom."

It was quiet for a long time.

"I'm here." Viv's voice trickled through the tiny speaker on Elijah's wrist.

"Viv, all of us are awake now. We're coming to get you," her mom insisted. "You saved us, Viv. We still have time to save you. You don't have to do this."

"I have to, Mom." Viv's voice crackled on the other end. "You know why."

Director Harlow's breath faltered, then determination filled her eyes.

"Well, I'm not letting them take you," she vowed.

Director Harlow jolted her arm toward Lieutenant Padilla, pulling a plasma pistol from his holster. She pointed it up toward the sky.

In one sudden movement, the Roswellian army tightened its circle above them, ready to lunge at any second. They weren't going to let anything get in the way of Megdar's plans.

Just as swiftly, Elijah put his hand on Director Harlow's wrist, stopping her dead in her tracks.

"Ms. Harlow," Elijah said softly. "You have to trust her. Trust *us*. We know what we're doing."

He stared intently at the director, his eyes boring into hers, as the Roswellians peered down at them. His gaze turned pleading, as if he was begging her to understand something.

After a long moment, Director Harlow's expression shifted and she seemed to deflate. A look of realization came over her face.

"I'm sorry," she huffed. "You're right. Viv trusts us, and we should trust her. Go. Bring them the key."

Elijah nodded, pushing down the last pang of fear. He popped Meekee up onto his shoulder.

"Hold on tight, little buddy," Elijah instructed.

Elijah activated the ignition on his flight suit, and the engine revved to life He clicked his heels and rocketed up into the air.

Eventually Elijah approached the edge of the Roswellian blockade. He nodded toward Meekee on his shoulder and showed the aliens that he was making a delivery. The army parted down the middle, allowing him to pass.

Elijah curved around the edge of the ship and zoomed into the upside-down cockpit, only to see Viv from behind as she floated in a field of harsh green light.

"Viv?" Elijah's voice trembled.

She turned around, still clutching her arm. When she recognized Elijah, a huge smile spread across her face, and despite everything, he couldn't help but smile back. He kicked the engine on his suit and sped toward her. Only a few more feet before he could wrap her in a hug.

At the last second, Megdar floated in between them.

"Good," Megdar smirked at Elijah. "You brought the key."

Elijah instinctively backed away. Viv just peeked out miserably from behind Megdar's back.

"I'll give you two a moment alone while I gather the others," Megdar said.

He floated across the cockpit to the control panel, leaving Viv and Elijah with some space to talk in private.

Elijah rushed toward Viv and threw his arms around her. "Are you okay? Did he hurt you?" he asked frantically.

"I'm okay, I'm okay," Viv assured him. "He's not an entirely bad person, Elijah. He's just tired. He wants to go home."

"Why did you agree to this? You know, your mom is right. Everyone's awake now," Elijah added. "We might have a shot at beating them if we all work together. Why does he even want you in the first place?"

"I can't explain everything now. Maybe one day . . ." Viv trailed off. "But not right now. You just have to trust me."

Elijah sighed, not liking that answer. He caught her green eyes with his deep stare.

"It's tough to do that when my only option is to never see you again," Elijah breathed. He suddenly realized this might be the last time they'd ever speak.

It seemed like Viv had realized this, too. She opened her mouth to talk, but before she could, Elijah leaned in close to whisper.

"Viv . . . Before you go, I wanted to tell you—"

"Meekee!" The tiny alien perched on his shoulder cut him off.

The little creature's interruption brought a chuckle out of the pair. "Right. I guess first you'll be needing this guy."

He handed Meekee over to Viv, and the tiny alien immediately cuddled up into Viv's hands lovingly, purring like a little green kitten.

All at once Megdar was standing right behind them.

"Vivian," Megdar interrupted. "It's time."

"Wait, no! I—" Elijah protested.

"It's okay, Elijah," Viv reassured him. "I'll be all right."

Elijah scooted around Megdar and wrapped Viv in his arms, his hand grasping at the back collar of her combat suit. He was careful not to put any pressure on her injured arm, but he still squeezed so tight that he thought his heart might burst.

Megdar tapped Elijah on the shoulder. "You might want to step back, boy," Megdar instructed.

Elijah pulled away from his hug with Viv, two tears streaming down the sides of his face. Viv looked stunned, and Elijah realized she had never seen him cry before.

Megdar held out his hand, moving Elijah backward with a gentle telekinetic push. Elijah ducked his head as Megdar led him out of the ship, being sure to flash Viv one last sad smile.

He heard Viv let out a whimper as she disappeared from sight.

Goodbye.

This is it.

Viv watched Elijah's jet-black hair vanish at the same time as Megdar's eyes began to glow with beams of neon green. His body became enveloped in the color as he extended both his arms and tensed his muscles.

In one swift motion, the entire ship flipped back to its upright position. Viv hovered in awe as the entire cockpit swiveled around before her eyes and she felt the hold of gravity shift and then restabilize.

His power is unimaginable.

Viv walked over to the glass window and peered down. Elijah descended toward the terrarium floor, joining the tiny specks of people on the ground.

Viv turned to face Megdar and almost had a heart attack at the sight. He was surrounded by the other Roswellians, all of them back in their monstrous true forms. There were dozens of them crammed into the ship, filling every inch of the cargo hold and the cockpit with slithering tentacles and ghastly bodies. They looked at Viv expectantly.

Using his telekinetic pull, Megdar floated Viv through the crowd of aliens and brought her to his side. She gathered that Megdar had told them who she was, and with all their hundreds of eyes gazing upon her, it almost seemed like she'd been accepted into this strange alien family.

"Would you like to do the honors?" Megdar motioned to the ship's dashboard.

A perfect Meekee-shaped hole glowed in the center of the control panel, with a slot for his little antenna and a holster for each of his tiny legs.

"Meekee!" the little alien exclaimed.

"Plug him in here, and we'll jump into hyperspace," Megdar said. "We'll be back on our home planet in no time. Would you like a churro for the commute?"

Viv just shook her head. She held Meekee steadily in the palm of her hand, steeling herself.

With a small push, she plugged the tiny alien into the dashboard, revving the ship's engines. Meekee locked into place with a loud click.

Viv took a deep breath and placed an unsteady hand on the back of her neck. She looked at Megdar and the other Roswellians.

Here we go.

A flash of black passed in front of her eyes.

Seconds later, the ship jumped into light speed and blasted out of the roof of the terrarium, disappearing into the night sky like a shooting star.

CHAPTER
TWENTY-FIVE

In a flash, the spaceship . . . and the Roswellians . . . were gone. And so was Viv. Elijah's mouth dropped open in shock.

"What happened?" Director Harlow yelled out. "Where's Viv?" She turned to Elijah.

"I—I don't know!" he stammered back.

"What do you mean? You said to trust you. I thought you had a plan!"

"I did have a plan. I planted a sonic grenade on her in the ship."

"A GRENADE?" Director Harlow yelled. "You blew up my daughter?"

"No! I thought it would transport her out of the ship, through one of those wormholes."

"And transport her where, exactly?"

"I don't know. Anywhere other than that ship. I thought she understood what I was doing!"

For a moment it was silent.

Then a look of pure despair fell over Director Harlow's face, and she clutched a trembling hand to her heart. Elijah's own heart broke in two.

It didn't work. Viv didn't realize the plan in time.

Charlotte draped her arm around Ray's shoulder as he struggled to hold back his own tears. Elijah craned his neck back and squinted toward the sky.

Viv . . . where are you?

The only thing he could see was the dusky light pouring in from above. The last of the other captured humans were finally waking up. Hundreds of Area 51 agents and their children huddled together in the center of the terrarium around Ray, Charlotte, and Elijah. Except for the dull sound of the wind that rustled through the terrarium sectors, it was silent.

Everything felt completely hopeless.

Charlotte curled into her dad's arms for a big hug. Her mother, not much of a hugger, gave her a soft pat on the head. Ray and Mr. Mond stood side by side, each using the other as support. Elijah collapsed into his father's arms, the exhaustion from all the adrenaline finally catching up to him.

She's gone. She's really gone.

Mr. Yates made his way to their circle.

"Director Harlow . . . I—I can't believe this . . . I can't believe any of this . . . What do we do now?"

Without saying a word, Director Harlow pulled a transmitter from her pocket and pressed a button. After a few minutes, a fleet of military-grade autopiloted Humvees from the compound garage rolled into the center of the terrarium to pick everyone up. After shuffling the rest of her employees and their dazed children safely into the cars, Director Harlow hopped into the backseat with the Monds, the Franks, and the Padillas.

The long ride back to the main hall was mostly silent. Elijah watched as Director Harlow stared out of the window for the entire ride. Instead of rattling off the story of their heroic battles and quick thinking to their parents, the kids kept to themselves. Even loudmouth Charlotte sniffled quietly in the corner.

Viv was gone.

It didn't feel real.

None of it felt real.

Driving through the underground compound, their Humvee passed by corridor after corridor of heavy locked doors hiding experimental rooms. Each hallway sent a shiver down Elijah's spine.

If the Roswellians were just in one of these holding cells, what other monsters and secrets could they be hiding here?

The fleet finally arrived at the main hall where the whole day had started. Elijah thought back to that morning, being welcomed at the compound by Director Harlow. It felt like a lifetime ago.

The main hall was almost unrecognizable. The walls were

blasted through with huge holes from plasma pistols. Shattered glass and crumbled concrete was littered across the floor. The Roswellians had certainly left their mark on this place.

The other employees arrived first. They stood in a semi-circle, woozy and still in a state of shock from being overtaken by the alien surprise attack. And they all clung tightly to their children; after the day's events, no one seemed to want to let each other go.

Much like how the Franks, Lieutenant Padilla, and Mr. Mond shuffled all of their kids out of the Humvee first, not willing to let them out of their sight.

Mr. Yates stepped out of his vehicle, shoulders tense and hunched, before yanking the door open on the other side for Director Harlow. She brushed off the dust and dirt on her skirt and took a few steps toward the miraculously still-standing podium.

Charlotte's father, Desmond, caught Director Harlow's wrist. "Cassandra, you don't have to speak right now," he whispered in her ear. "I can't imagine what you're going through."

"I can handle it," Director Harlow replied. Her voice was forced but steady. "These people are counting on me. We still have a job to do."

Director Harlow climbed the steps and took her spot at the podium. Two hundred employees, agents, and children looked on fearfully, waiting for direction.

She adjusted the microphone and cleared her throat.

"What happened here today was a tragedy," she began. "But I assure you that everyone's safety is still my top priority. For everyone who showed up here today for the first time, I'm sure this has all been a huge shock, and I'm so sorry you had to experience all this. But for everyone else, we knew the security risks of working at a place like Area 51. And yes, we got to witness those dangers firsthand today. But we were also very lucky to have had a few special guests to save our butts when we needed them."

Director Harlow gazed at the three kids huddled by their parents. Elijah knew he, Charlotte, and Ray should try to put on a brave face for everyone else, but it was all they could do to keep the tears in.

Director Harlow took a deep breath and looked down at the podium.

"And though . . . and although my dear daughter, Vivian, has been taken from me," she said, her hands gripping the podium for support, "we will not be giving up on her."

The crowd began to whisper and murmur. Director Harlow leaned in closer to the microphone.

"In all the years I've worked at this compound, we've never lost a single person," she said. "And our mission remains the same—to improve life here on Earth through science and innovation. But maybe, somewhere along the way, we got a little distracted and forgot our promises. Now I promise you it's time to correct that.

"Regardless of how afraid you all might be feeling right now, we have in front of us a new mission," she continued. "In this very room, we have gathered some of the brightest minds in the world. We *will* figure out how to get my daughter back, no matter—"

A sharp sound chirped up, cutting Director Harlow's sentence short. Everyone in the room went silent, remembering the last time a sound like that had rung out through the main hall.

Elijah looked down at his wrist communicator. The orange screen lit up in short bursts.

A call was coming in.

No way . . .

It could only mean one thing. Elijah tried to press the button on his wrist and answer the call, but the button wouldn't budge.

"It's not working!" Elijah said.

Charlotte leaned over to take a look at it. "The button's jammed. We need something small, something sharp," she explained. She and Elijah started frantically looking for an object that fit that description, while recognition of the situation slowly started to dawn on the adults' faces.

"Wait a second!" Ray said suddenly. He began slapping at the front of his chest, still covered in sewage and mud.

"Ray, not now—"

"Got it!" he said. In his hand, miraculously still intact, was the pen he'd taken from the Gadgets Room all those hours ago. "Told you it would come in handy!"

Charlotte wasted no time. She grabbed the pen and wedged it beneath the button. Sure enough, it worked, mud and all.

On the tiny screen on Elijah's wrist, Viv's face shimmered in dusky, orange light. Behind her, he could just make out the last remnants of a beautiful sunset dipping beyond the edge of the lake behind her. Faintly, he could hear what sounded like other students from Groom Lake Middle School in the background, bombarding her with questions about the crazy purple combat suit she was still wearing.

Viv looked down into the camera on her own wrist and flashed a cheeky smile.

"So are you guys coming to the lake or what?"

"Viv?" Elijah's eyes lit up with joy.

"What?" Ray exclaimed. "You're ALIVE? How did you get to the lake?"

Director Harlow jumped down from the podium, pushed past other employees, and beelined toward the three kids huddled together.

Elijah let out a burst of laughter. "Oh my GOSH! I can't believe it worked! You found the grenade?"

"Yes!" Viv said, her voice crackly through the speaker. "Right before the ship jumped into light speed, I pulled the pin on the grenade. Looks like even Area 51 tech likes the lake, because after I felt my molecules stop rearranging, I found myself here!"

Charlotte slapped her forehead in amazement. For once, she was speechless.

"But that plan was insane!" Ray called out.

"It was insane, but just the right amount of insane!" Viv said.

"Vivian?" Director Harlow called out frantically.

"I'm here, Mom! I'm fine!" Viv replied from the tiny speaker.

The entire audience erupted into applause. Everyone from agents to kids cheered in pure joy at the sound of Viv's voice.

Elijah couldn't hold it in any longer, and he burst into tears of relief. His dad put his arm around his shoulder and held him close.

Elijah turned to Charlotte and Ray. "Don't tell anybody about this," he threatened between heavy sobs.

Ray laughed, then turned when Charlotte tapped his shoulder.

"I've got another surprise for you," she said.

Charlotte clutched something hidden in her hands behind her back. She pulled her arms around and uncurled her palms.

"Meekee!"

The tiny alien jumped out of Charlotte's hands and clung to Ray's face in a big bear hug.

"What?" Ray exclaimed, peeling his overexcited little friend off his nose. "Meekee! My baby boy!"

"Yep! In that last hug before he left, I cloned the little guy with the last bit of juice in the gauntlets," Charlotte said happily. "The real Meekee was here on the ground all along!"

Holding Meekee in his hands, Ray started to cry, too. "Oh man!" He sniffled. "I thought I'd never see you again, buddy! I haven't even taught you how to read yet!"

"Meekee!" The tiny alien purred in delight.

Ray turned to Elijah and leaned in close to his ear. "But, Elijah? What if that grenade didn't go off like you planned and Viv was still trapped on the ship?" Ray asked.

"And what if a meteorite crashed into my butt?" Elijah said. "Don't worry about it, Ray! Everything worked out. Viv is safe. You get to keep Meekee. Everyone's happy!"

"Guys—" Viv's voice came in through the speaker. "There's something else I need to tell you . . ."

"What is it? Are you okay?" Director Harlow said.

"This was no accident. Someone helped the Roswellians with their plan. *Somebody who works at Area 51.*"

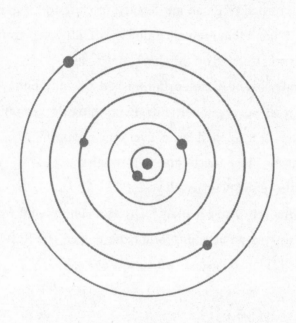

CHAPTER
TWENTY-SIX

Director Harlow stood frozen in shock.

Could someone at Area 51 really be a traitor?

"What do you mean, Viv?" she asked, peering around the crowd of her employees suspiciously. Everyone in the circle tensed up.

"In the ship," Viv replied, "Megdar told me that this plan was a long time in the making. Someone from the inside was helping him."

Director Harlow's fists clenched by her sides. Someone had betrayed her.

"Brooks—Brooks, where are you?" She turned to her left. Mr. Yates stepped forward from the audience. "Get me a list of every employee who accessed subsector 413 in the past few weeks."

"Yes, ma'am, of course. Right away." He nodded, already scurrying toward the door.

At the sound of his voice, Charlotte's eyes opened wide.

"HOLD ON A SECOND!"

"What is it, Charlotte?" Mr. Frank asked.

"That voice! It's him!" Charlotte pointed at Mr. Yates. "*He's* the one I heard talking to Megdar from the airshaft!"

"Wait a second," Elijah said. "Charlotte . . . *He's* the one you heard talking to Megdar? After everyone else had been knocked out?"

"Yes! I'm sure of it. I never forget a voice!"

Mr. Yates laughed. "Surely, I have no idea what this young lady is talking about. I was knocked out unconscious just like the rest of you. Cassandra, I'll just go get that information you asked for . . ."

"Wait," Viv piped in through Elijah's wrist. "Megdar said Take Your Kids to Work Day was all part of their plan, too. That was your idea, wasn't it, Mr. Yates?"

"It . . . uh . . ."

"Yes . . . it was," Director Harlow remembered. "I did think it was strange that you didn't bring your own children . . ."

"M-my children are just too young, like I said, I didn't have anything to do w—"

"TAKE HIS SHOES OFF!" Ray shouted.

Everyone stopped and turned to look at the muddy mess of a boy missing his pants.

"Ray? What do you mean?" Elijah asked.

"My shoes? What on earth is this kid talking about?" Mr. Yates said, still trying to inch toward the door.

"When I was tiny, I fell into a really stinky shoe! The stinky shoe of somebody who was working with Megdar. I heard them talking about leaving together on the ship!"

Director Harlow looked at Ray with confusion.

"I promise! I'm telling the truth. My nose knows. Gimme that stanky foot, and I can prove it."

Mr. Yates stared out at the group.

"You've gotta be kidding me," he said. "You're gonna take this kid's word over mine? He's not even wearing pants!"

"I'm sorry, Brooks. But I have to ask you to take your shoes off," Director Harlow said.

He scoffed. "You really want to smell my *shoes*?"

Director Harlow just furrowed her brow in response.

"Fine! Fine!" He bent down and pulled off one of his dress shoes. "But honestly, this is ridiculous!"

He handed the loafer to Director Harlow. She took a quick sniff. The smell was repugnant.

She handed the shoe to Elijah, who took a huge whiff.

"Ugh! Yuck! Geez Louise! You weren't kidding, Ray!" Elijah said. "This thing really does stink!"

"Okay, so my feet smell!" Mr. Yates admitted. "That doesn't mean I helped a horde of aliens escape! These kids don't know what they're talking about. They don't have any hard evidence."

The sting of his minty breath stung Director Harlow's eyes.

"What about that mud stain on your sock?" Ray pointed

to the smudge peeking out from Mr. Yates's ankle. "The stain that's shaped exactly like my miniature body!"

"Meekee!" the tiny alien shouted in support.

"Yeah! And what about these?" Elijah dug into the pocket of his flight suit and pulled out a rattling box of mints. "These Tic Tacs! I found them in the Gadgets Room!"

"Oh, come on, now. I'm not the only person here who still eats Tic Tacs!"

Director Harlow raised an eyebrow and looked around at her employees.

"Does anyone else here eat Tic Tacs every day?" she asked.

Everyone in the crowd shook their heads in unison: No.

Mr. Yates shifted from side to side.

Suddenly, he pushed a pack of employees out of the way and took off running, hobbling away in his one shoe.

"Somebody stop him!" Director Harlow called out.

But before anyone could make a move, Mr. Mond had already fired the O.D.O.R. in Mr. Yates's direction. "Got him!"

The noxious green fart cloud swelled around Mr. Yates's face. With one deep inhale, his eyes rolled back into his head and his body hit the ground with a thud.

Director Harlow rushed over to him.

"But why, Brooks?" Director Harlow asked as his last bits of consciousness faded away. "Why would you go work with the Roswellians and plan something like this?"

The smell of the O.D.O.R. around him was even worse

than his shoes. Mr. Yates's eyes could barely stay open. She crouched down, getting close enough to him for no one else to hear.

"I did it for . . . for science . . . ," he muttered. "I did it for the same reason as you . . . I saw what you did to Megdar all those years ago, how you took what you wanted . . . I saw the security footage of you getting his sample and then injecting yourself in the lab . . . The footage you tried to delete . . . I put the pieces together myself . . . He was going to take me to their planet, Cassandra . . . I would've been the first person . . . the first human to live among an alien species . . . to have their powers . . . No one was supposed to get hurt . . . But they lied to me . . ."

Director Harlow shut her eyes. She understood now.

He's just like I was.

She'd once been a young scientist, too. Desperate to make her mark on the world and not caring who she hurt to make it happen. Stealing Megdar's DNA and lying to him about it . . . It was a mistake that haunted her to this day, and one she'd spent most of her life trying to make amends for. But now, she realized, she'd clearly not done enough.

She took a deep breath and did what she had to do now.

"Al, take him away."

"Yes, ma'am!" Mr. Mond said, gladly picking Mr. Yates up off the floor.

"Brooks, I'm sorry." Director Harlow sighed. "But you're fired."

As Mr. Mond led the barely conscious man out of the main hall, the other employees and agents cheered all around them. It was all over.

Ray looked up at Director Harlow with a smile full of braces, and she couldn't help but lean over and give him a big hug.

I'm so proud of these kids. They all saved Area 51.

Viv sat on the shore of the lake, staring out across the water. The pain in her arm was still there but beginning to fade away—like the last inches of sun sinking beyond the Nevada mountains.

She looked down at the tiny screen on her busted wrist communicator, watching as her friends were celebrated like true heroes.

A contented smile spread across her face.

She might not be headed to another planet, and she would have to learn to control her powers on her own, but if there was anything she learned over the course of the entire day, it was this:

With my friends by my side, I can do anything.

CHAPTER
TWENTY-SEVEN

Viv and Elijah relaxed on the couch in the Harlows' living room, watching Ray and Charlotte ferociously packing bags for their long-awaited trip to the lake.

"Dibs on the blue towel!" Ray shouted.

"Fine, but you have to carry the umbrella," Charlotte argued.

"No way! It's too heavy."

"Ray, you caught two hundred people falling out of a spaceship yesterday," Charlotte pointed out. "I think you can handle an umbrella."

Viv leaned against the side of a sofa cushion. The TV was droning on at a low volume from on top of the mantel. An international news reporter was on-screen, frantically describing a freak incident in Cleveland yesterday in which a seemingly *very realistic* animatronic *T. rex* materialized out of nowhere and crushed an entire row of empty houses. Luckily, the reporter said, no one had been injured, and the animatronic had been quickly cleared away by an unnamed government clean-up crew.

Viv reached across the couch for the remote control to click the TV off. Her elbow accidentally knocked a pair of sunglasses off the armrest and flung them behind the sofa. She rubbed her arm, feeling a twinge of soreness still lingering above her wrist.

Yesterday, after the Humvee picked her up from the lake, Viv was brought back to the compound, where a team of doctors from Area 51 injected a rapidly reforming bone serum into her injured arm. The nurse administering the shot explained how the serum was still technically undergoing experimental trials, but she promised that it would either heal her arm within a few hours or turn her bones into Popsicle sticks.

So far, it looked like she was Popsicle-free.

Charlotte lugged her guitar case into the front hallway, her flip-flops smacking across the tile floors.

"Charlotte, are you sure you wanna bring your guitar to the lake?" Elijah asked. "It might get wet."

"The sandier my feet are, the better grip I'll have with my toes," Charlotte explained. "It's the perfect place to practice."

Elijah rolled his eyes. He tossed a bottle of sunscreen into Ray's bag, but it bounced off a beach ball and smacked Ray in the arm.

"Ouch! Watch it!"

Viv smiled, watching her friends get ready on this perfect summer day. She took a deep breath and looked down at her hands. She focused on each inch of skin, checking for even the slightest hue of green.

Nothing.

Viv let out a sigh of relief. She glanced back up at the faces of her friends.

They didn't know anything yet. And they would never know, not if she had anything to do with it.

Elijah and Charlotte laughed at the splotches of sunscreen dripping off Ray's nose, blissfully unaware that they were sitting in a room with a half-human, half-alien twelve-year-old.

Viv buried her hands under the towel in her lap. She wanted to curl up and disappear, but for now, being careful would have to do. She was just glad Mr. Yates hadn't let anything slip before he was taken into custody. While she had been in the Area 51 infirmary, she overheard how his interrogation had revealed that Mr. Yates had been trying to take initiative and go through old video files of the Roswellians when he'd stumbled upon the footage of her mother and Megdar. His lifelong dream of traveling to space led him to sneak into the Roswellians' sector to bribe Megdar with the information, and together they had hatched their scheme. All it had taken was planning out the Take Your Kids to Work Day, and the rest was history.

At this point, Viv wasn't focused on how the events of yesterday had come together. As long as she could keep her powers a secret, her life could still be perfectly normal. She made a promise to herself:

This summer can still be fun.

Trips to the lake, late-night ice cream runs, long bike rides under the Nevada sun. In three months, high school would roll around in the fall and then Viv could really disappear. Elijah would be on his way to joining the military academy, Charlotte would be at music school, and Ray would be winning science fairs at Groom Lake High.

By then, I'll be someone else's problem.

"How long until your mom gets home, Viv?" Charlotte asked, snapping Viv out of her daydream. "We're gonna miss high tide!"

"No clue," Viv sighed. "She hasn't answered any of my—"

A sharp chirping sound rang out from the kitchen. Everyone's head whipped around.

Viv's wrist com vibrated against the countertop.

Someone was calling.

In a flash, all four kids crowded around the countertop, staring down at the intimidating cracked device.

Viv reached out slowly and pressed the answer button. The screen lit up with Director Harlow's face.

Viv gritted her teeth. For the first time in her life, she had no idea what to say to her mother.

"Hello, kids!" Director Harlow called out from the center of the Area 51 terrarium. "Hope you're all recovering after the eventful day yesterday!"

"Hi, Director Harlow!" Ray beamed. "How are things going at the base?"

"Oh, you know," she said with a grin. "Slowly putting things back together. And I had to place an order for some new DNA scanners for the VERT train to replace the few you kids sneezed all over . . ."

Charlotte and Elijah shared an uneasy glance.

"Are we . . . in trouble?" Ray asked sheepishly.

"No, you're not in trouble," Director Harlow said. "But many of the other parents suggested that we wipe your memories. Make you forget about this whole thing like it never happened. Just like what we did with the other employees' children who were there . . . and your schoolmates at the lake who saw Viv in that combat suit . . ."

The kids all looked at each other with nervous expressions.

"Really?" Charlotte asked. "And are you going to?"

"No, no. We've decided not to wipe your memories . . . At least not *yet*." Director Harlow joked. "Because what you kids did yesterday showed real bravery and courage, and it didn't seem right to erase those moments in your lives. I was very impressed with your quick thinking. We all were."

Viv felt a knot form in her stomach hearing this praise coming from her mom. She still hadn't confronted her mom about the truth.

Director Harlow cleared her throat and continued. "I know you all were supposed to finally get that trip to the lake together today, but I have something more important to discuss with you . . ." She trailed off.

"We'd like to offer each of you an internship for the summer."

Elijah's jaw fell open. Charlotte's eyes widened.

"An internship?" Ray asked. "Where?"

"At Area 51, of course!" Director Harlow smiled. "I want you all working here full-time."

Viv couldn't believe her ears.

What? Did I hear that right?

"I don't understand . . . ," Viv said.

"Yeah, me neither," Charlotte added. "We basically destroyed your entire office yesterday."

"Oh, don't worry about that," Director Harlow said.

"But why, Mom?"

"Well, if I'm being honest . . . What the four of you accomplished yesterday was very impressive. With your quick thinking, you managed to pull off things that most seasoned agents couldn't even dare to do. Like you, Charlotte."

Her ears perked up at the sound of her name.

"Charlotte, no one else has been able to use those duplicator gauntlets the way you did. The way you had complete control over all those clones was incredible. And, Elijah, your flying abilities were top-notch. Nearly as good as your own dad's. Not to mention that your last-minute plan with that sonic grenade saved Viv's life. And, Ray . . . you fought off a *T. rex* and caught us all when we were falling. You were very brave."

"Aw. Gee, thanks, Director Harlow," he replied.

Director Harlow paused for a moment.

"And, Viv," she continued. "If it weren't for you, we'd all be floating in space right now. Your leadership and resilience saved our lives. You were willing to sacrifice yourself to save all of us, and this base. I'm very, very proud of you."

Vivian blushed at her mom's words.

"The point is—this internship is a once-in-a-lifetime opportunity. I think, under our watchful eyes, we can turn you four into fantastic agents one day."

"Wow. An internship? Does Area 51 even *do* internships?" Elijah wondered aloud.

"Well, we do now!" Director Harlow exclaimed. "Of course, we'll need to get all of you the proper security clearance and badges. There's quite a bit of paperwork to get done, but after that, you'll have full access to the compound in case we need your help with anything."

Elijah, Charlotte, and Ray looked at each other with growing smiles.

Viv felt a bittersweet wave pass over her.

An internship . . . I mean, that sounds cool. But what about my perfect summer?

"Speaking of, we're still having trouble closing one of the wormholes you kids ripped open yesterday," Director Harlow replied, adjusting the view of the camera.

She ducked out of frame.

Behind her, a black wormhole swirled and sparkled in the air. Agents and employees stood with weapons at the ready.

In a rush of iron and armor, medieval knights atop horses came pouring out of the rip in the space-time continuum. Their swords clashed against the trees of the prehistoric forest. The agents fought back, but the army of knights plowed across the jungle.

Ray's jaw hit the floor.

"Wait . . ." He folded his arms over his chest. "You're telling me time travel is real?"

"Well . . . yes. Of course it is," Director Harlow said.

Ray eyes opened wide, and he jutted his finger at Charlotte. "HAHA! I knew it! TOLD you! Ms. Harlow, have you ever met Leonardo da Vinci?"

"Ray, focus! I hate to say it, but I need you all to come in today," Director Harlow yelled over the noise. "Like, now. We could really use your help."

A honk from outside echoed through the house. Ray, Charlotte, and Elijah rushed over to the window and peered out.

A self-driving Area 51 Humvee was parked in the driveway, one door open. The camouflaging tiles on the car's exterior twisted and spun to match the morning sky above, activating the vehicle's stealth mode.

"Whoa! Cool!" Ray shouted.

Elijah turned back to the wrist com on the counter. "We're on our way, Director Harlow!"

"Excellent. See you all soon."

The screen cut to black. Viv stared helplessly at her own reflection in the small square of glass where her mother's smiling face had just disappeared.

Elijah, Charlotte, and Ray threw off their towels, dropped their beach bags, and scurried toward the door.

"Wait!" Viv cried out.

But she was too late. They were already bounding down the porch steps toward the car.

Viv chased them out the front door as they all piled into the backseat of the Humvee. She ducked her head in, bracing herself against the frame.

"Hold on, guys!" Viv hesitated. "You really want to go back there?"

The three friends stopped buckling their seat belts for a moment and looked up at her in disbelief.

"Of course!" Charlotte said. "What? You're saying that you don't?"

Viv looked down at her feet.

"I mean, uh . . . I don't know," Viv mumbled. Images from yesterday were burned into her mind. The monstrous Roswellians. The roar of the *T. rex*'s jaws inches from their faces. Megdar's creepy smile and the way he seemed to know everything about her.

"You guys aren't scared at all?" Viv asked.

"Maybe a little," Elijah admitted. "But we already made it

through yesterday. Can't get much worse than that."

"Speak for yourself," Charlotte said, smacking Elijah on the arm. "I'm not scared. And I don't know what you heard, but it sounded to me like our parents need our help."

"Ray?" Viv asked. "Even you? You want to do this?"

"Come on, Viv. You know this is my dream!" Ray piped up. "An internship at Area 51? I can't imagine a better way to start off my career in science. Plus, that O.D.O.R. weapon needs my expertise. No one knows farts better than me."

"Plus, we'll all be together. What better way to spend our last summer before high school?" Elijah asked.

"So what do you say, Viv? Are you up for it?" Elijah smiled at her, his deep brown eyes sparkling in the sunlight, hand outstretched.

Viv took a deep breath. She thought about what Megdar had said to her back on the spaceship.

You'll never be able to understand your powers on your own.

If she wanted to know the truth about herself, the truth about her past, the truth about everything . . . Area 51 was the place to go.

In three months, regardless of what happened this summer, her whole life would change.

Maybe having a few more adventures at Area 51 isn't such a bad idea after all. Besides, I did want to spend the summer with my friends . . . It's my last chance.

Viv grabbed Elijah's hand and pulled herself into the backseat.

"All right, Viv!" Ray smiled, patting her on the shoulder.

Viv reached over and clicked her seat belt, then leaned forward toward the front of the car.

"Take us to Area 51," Viv said to the driverless Humvee. It beeped in affirmation.

The engine rumbled to life, and the automatic steering wheel locked into place. Its tires screeched across the pavement as the massive vehicle pulled out of the driveway and onto the street.

"Woo! Yeah!" Charlotte cheered. "Let's go kick some medieval butt!"

The invisible Humvee soared around the other cars on the road like a hawk cutting its wings through the breeze, going completely unnoticed.

In the back corner, Charlotte and Ray geeked out about all the new tech and weapons they were going to test once they got back to the base.

Viv looked down at her hands.

Still no green.

She turned toward Elijah sitting next to her, watching his eyes light up in awe with each quick navigational turn the autopilot system made.

She built up the courage and tapped him gently on the shoulder.

"So . . . ," Viv whispered. "What is it you were going to say to me on the ship? Before Megdar cut you off?"

Elijah's cheeks turned bright pink. He looked out the window, lifting his hand to scratch the back of his head.

"Oh, um . . . ," Elijah mumbled, turning toward Viv. "I'll tell you another time . . . I promise."

"Okay," she chuckled. "If you say so . . ."

Elijah smiled at her. She smiled back.

Viv turned away, feeling a burning in her cheeks. She didn't want Elijah to see her blushing, too.

She stared out the car window, watching rows of suburban houses disappear behind them, until something caught her attention.

In the reflection of the glass, she could see what was actually warming the skin on her face.

It wasn't her cheeks blushing.

It was her eyes . . .

They were *glowing bright green.*

ACKNOWLEDGMENTS

JAMES S. MURRAY

First and foremost, I would like to thank my multitalented writing partner Carsen Smith, without whom this book series would not be possible. Thanks to our excellent colleagues at Penguin—Rob Valois, Francesco Sedita, Alex Wolfe, Lizzie Goodell, and the entire team that brought Area 51 Interns to life. Thanks to my colleagues Joseph, Nicole, and Ethan. Thanks to Jack Rovner and Dexter Scott from Vector Management, Brandi Bowles from UTA, Danny Passman from GTRB, Phil Sarna and Mitch Pearlstein from PSBM, and Elena Stokes and the excellent team from Wunderkind PR. And special thanks to Brad Meltzer and R. L. Stine. Mom and Dad and my entire family, I love you all. And most importantly, thanks to my amazing wife, Melyssa, whose endless love and support makes everything worthwhile. Finally, thanks to all the young *Impractical Jokers* fans around the world. Remember—if Vivian and her friends can overcome an alien attack on Area 51, there's nothing you can't do as well!

CARSEN SMITH

An absurdly enormous thank-you to our miraculous team at Penguin Workshop—Francesco Sedita, Rob Valois, and Alex Wolfe—for believing in this project and making the book better every step of the way. Special shout-out to Alex, a longtime friend and now a lifelong collaborator. To Brandi Bowles at UTA, everyone at Vector, Petur Antonsson for bringing these characters to life, and the incredible team at Impractical Productions. To my entire family, thank you for the nonstop support. To my Aunt Jil and Papa, whose boundless creativity has me hopeful that imagination is genetic. To Mom and Dad, every other thank-you is smaller than the one for you two. Please don't ground me. To Will, the real-life Ray and my best friend. I love you and thanks for playing guitar in my ear every time I had to write. Of course, a huge thank-you to my coauthor James. None of this would be possible without you and your constant drive to create. You've been an invaluable mentor, a sublime creative partner, and a phenomenal friend over the years. And if any aliens eventually read this book, give me a call. I'd love to buy you a coffee.

JOIN THE

AREA·51 INTERNS

IN THEIR SECOND ADVENTURE, *ZONED OUT!*

Viv, Charlotte, Elijah, and Ray may be official interns at Area 51, but their parents don't seem to trust them enough to do more than file paperwork. Luckily, Elijah discovers a map to a secret Forbidden Zone, and the group jumps at the chance to explore the mysterious place that houses some of the most elusive monsters on Earth. But after the Chupacabra, Loch Ness Monster, and more terrifying creatures escape, they'll have to prove themselves to their parents and capture the beasts to save the base!